THE LOGAN TWINS

Twin brothers Ben and Jake Logan have each become wildly successful in their own way, and yet they're still getting into trouble together. This time it's when they're sailing off the coast of New Zealand and a massive storm hits, tearing their boat apart…

But the Logan brothers aren't beaten easily. And when they find themselves on very different shores neither of them knows just how much the storm—and the strong, irresistible women they meet in the heart of it—will change their lives for ever!

Available in June 2014
NINE MONTHS TO CHANGE HIS LIFE
by Marion Lennox

And don't miss
THE MAVERICK MILLIONAIRE
by Alison Roberts
available in July 2014

Dear Reader

New Zealand's Bay of Islands has to be one of the most beautiful places on earth. The bay is a mass of tiny islands—some inhabited, most not. Kayaking round the bay, often surrounded by dolphins, I land in places that take my breath away.

'But it's not always like this,' the locals tell me. 'When the wind gets up it can be frightening.' So the author in me looks out over the dotted islands, at the yachts on the sparkling waters, at the isolation of the place, and thinks: *What if...?*

As luck would have it my Kiwi author mate Alison Roberts is also enchanted with the Bay of Islands, so we've '*What if-ed*' together. What if we had an international super-yacht race and a cyclone? What if we had two bad-boy brothers sailing from New York? What if we used this setting to transform four lives...?

We've had a wonderful time throwing sexy, dramatic and tender and fun ingredients into our pot of two linked stories. May you have as much enjoyment reading as we did writing them.

Marion Lennox

NINE MONTHS TO
CHANGE HIS LIFE

BY
MARION LENNOX

Published in Great Britain 2014
by Mills & Boon, an imprint of Harlequin (UK) Limited,
Eton House, 18-24 Paradise Road, Richmond, Surrey, TW9 1SR

© 2014 Marion Lennox

ISBN: 978 0 263 24245 4

Harlequin (UK) Limited's policy is to use papers that are natural,
renewable and recyclable products and made from wood grown in
sustainable forests. The logging and manufacturing processes conform
to the legal environmental regulations of the country of origin.

Printed and bound in Great Britain
by CPI Antony Rowe, Chippenham, Wiltshire

Marion Lennox is a country girl, born on an Australian dairy farm. She moved on—mostly because the cows just weren't interested in her stories! Married to a 'very special doctor', Marion writes for the Mills & Boon® Medical Romance™ and Mills & Boon® Cherish™ lines. (She used a different name for each category for a while—readers looking for her past romance titles should search for author Trisha David as well). She's now had more than seventy-five romance novels accepted for publication.

In her non-writing life Marion cares for kids, cats, dogs, chooks and goldfish. She travels, she fights her rampant garden (she's losing) and her house dust (she's lost). Having spun in circles for the first part of her life, she's now stepped back from her 'other' career, which was teaching statistics at her local university. Finally she's reprioritised her life, figured out what's important and discovered the joys of deep baths, romance and chocolate. Preferably all at the same time!

Recent books by Marion Lennox:

CHRISTMAS AT THE CASTLE
SPARKS FLY WITH THE BILLIONAIRE
A BRIDE FOR THE MAVERICK MILLIONAIRE**
HER OUTBACK RESCUER**
MARDIE AND THE CITY SURGEON*
NIKKI AND THE LONE WOLF*
MISTY AND THE SINGLE DAD*
ABBY AND THE BACHELOR COP*
CHRISTMAS WITH HER BOSS

*Banksia Bay
**Journey Through the Outback

**These and other titles by Marion Lennox
are available in eBook format
from www.millsandboon.co.uk**

CHAPTER ONE

FROM THE MOMENT they were born, the Logan boys were trouble.

They were dark-haired, dark-eyed and full of mischief. Usually ignored by their wealthy, emotionally distant parents, they ran their nannies ragged and they ran themselves ragged. There wasn't a lot they wouldn't dare each other to do.

As they grew to men, tall, tough and ripped, their risks escalated. Some of those risks turned out to be foolish, Ben conceded. Joining the army and going to Afghanistan had been foolish. Back in civvies, attempting to get on with their careers, the trauma was still with them.

Sailing round the world to distract Jake from his failed marriage had also turned out to be stupid. Especially now, as Cyclone Lila bore down on their frail life raft, as one harness hung free from the chopper overhead.

'Take Ben first,' Jake yelled to the paramedic who'd been lowered with the harness, but Ben wasn't buying it.

'I'm the eldest,' Ben snapped. He was only older by twenty minutes but the responsibility of that twenty minutes had weighed on him all his life. 'Go.'

Jake refused, but the woman swinging from the chopper was risking all to save them. The weather was crazy—no one should be on the sea in such conditions. Arguing had to be done hard and fast.

He did what he had to do. The things he said to get Jake to go first were unforgivable—but he got the harness on.

'The chopper's full,' the paramedic yelled at Ben as she signalled for the chopper to pull them free. 'We'll come back for you as soon as we can.'

Or not. They all knew how unlikely another rescue was. The cyclone had veered erratically from its predicted path, catching the whole yachting fleet unprepared. The speed at which it was travelling was breathtaking, and there was no escape. Massive waves had smashed their boat, and they were still on the edge of the cyclone. The worst was yet to come.

At least Jake was safe—he hoped. The wind was making the rope from the chopper swing wildly, hurling Jake and the paramedic through the cresting waves. *Get up there,* he pleaded silently. *Move.*

Then the next wave bore down, a monster of breaking foam. He saw it coming, slammed down the hatch of the life raft and held on for dear life as the sea tossed his flimsy craft like a beach ball in surf.

We'll come back for you as soon as we can.

When the cyclone was over?

The wave passed and he dared open the hatch a little. The chopper was higher, but Jake and his rescuer were still swinging.

'Stay safe, brother,' he whispered. 'Stay safe until I see you again.'

A cyclone was heading straight for him. *Until I see you again...* What a bitter joke.

This was no mere storm. This was a cyclone, and in a cyclone there could surely be few worse places to be than on Hideaway Island.

Hideaway Island was tiny, a dot on the outer edge of the Bay of Islands off New Zealand's north coast. Two of Mary's friends, a surgeon and his lawyer wife, had bought it for a song years ago. They'd built a hut in the centre of the island and bought a serviceable boat to ferry themselves back and forth to the mainland. They'd decided it was paradise.

But Henry and Barbara now had impressive professional lives and three children. They hardly ever made it out here. It'd been on the market for a year, but with the global financial crisis no one was buying.

Right now, Henry and Barbara were in New York, but before they'd left, Henry had tossed Mary the keys to the hut and boat.

'You might use some solitude until this fuss dies down,' Henry told her with rough kindness. 'Could you check on the place while we're away? Stay if you like; we'd be grateful. It might be what you need.'

It was what she needed. Henry was one of the few who didn't blame her. Hideaway had seemed a reasonable place to run.

Until today. Heinz, her terrier-size, fifty-seven-or-more-variety dog, was looking at her as if he was worried, and his worry was justified. The wind was escalating by the minute. Outside the trees were bending and groaning with its force, and the roughly built hut felt distinctly unstable.

'We could end up in Texas,' Mary muttered, shaking her useless radio. Had a transmission tower fallen in the wind? Her phone was dead and there was no radio reception.

At six this morning the radio had said Cyclone Lila was five hundred miles off the coast, veering north-east instead of in its predicted northern trajectory. There was concern for a major international yacht race, but there'd been no hint that it might turn south and hit the Bay of Islands. Residents of New Zealand's north had merely been advised that the outside edges could cause heavy winds.

'Tie down outside furniture,' the broadcast had said. 'Don't park under trees.'

That was a normal storm warning—nothing to worry about. Mary had thought briefly of taking the boat and heading for the mainland, but the wind was rising and the usually placid sea around the islands was rough. It'd be safer to sit it out.

Or it had seemed safer, until about an hour ago.

Another gust slammed into the hut. A sheet of iron ripped from the roof and sleet swept inside.

The foundations creaked and the pictures on the wall swayed.

Uh-oh.

'I think we might head for the cave,' she told Heinz uneasily. 'You want a walk?'

The little terrier-cum-beagle-cum-a-lot-of-other-things cocked his head and looked even more worried. Right now a walk didn't appeal even to Heinz.

But the cave was appealing. Mary and Heinz had explored it a couple of days ago. It was wide and deep, set in the cliffs above the only beach where swimming was possible. Best of all, it faced west. It'd protect them from the worst of the gale.

Now that the roof was open, there didn't seem to be a choice. She had to go, and go now before it got worse. But what to take? The cave was only two or three hundred yards away. There was a flattish track and she had a trolley, the one Barbara and Henry used to lug supplies from boat to hut.

The boat. There was a sickening thought. The tiny natural harbour on the east of the island should protect the boat in all but the worst conditions—but these were the worst conditions.

She had no communications. No boat. She was on her own.

So what else was new? She'd been on her own now for as long as she could remember. Like it or not, she'd learned to depend entirely on herself, and she could do it now.

Concentrate on practicalities.

She grabbed plastic garbage bags and started stuffing things inside. Provisions, dog food, firestarters, kindling, bedding. Her manuscript. That was a joke, but she was taking it anyway.

Water containers. What else? What would Barbara and Henry want her to save?

Barbara's patchwork quilt? The lovely cushions embroidered by Barbara's grandmother? They went into plastic bags, too.

Another sheet of roofing iron went flying. The cottage was now totally open to the weather.

She had to stop. This was starting to be seriously scary and she had to pull the trolley.

'Why couldn't you be a sled dog?' she demanded of Heinz as she hauled open the door and faced the weather. 'You could help me pull.'

In answer, Heinz stared up at the wildly swaying trees, jumped onto the trolley and wriggled down among the plastic bags.

He was terrified. So was Mary, but she made herself pause. She made herself think. What else might be important?

'First-aid kit,' she muttered, and headed back into the already soaking cottage to find her medical bag. As a district nurse she still had it with her, and she'd brought it to the island just in case.

In case of splinters. In case of colds in the head. Not in case of cyclones.

She could hear branches splintering from the trees. There was no time for more.

And then the rest of the roof peeled off, with a shriek of tin against tin.

'Go,' she muttered, and started pulling. Heavy didn't begin to describe it. Sleet was stinging her eyes, her face, every part of her.

What to discard? Everything but essentials? Nothing Barbara and Henry cherished?

'Don't be a wuss,' she told herself. 'They entrusted you with their island. The least you can do is save their stuff. The path's reasonably flat. Come on, muscles, pull.'

She tugged and the trolley moved.

'I can do this,' she said through gritted teeth, and put her head down into the wind and pulled.

The life raft was in freefall. Ben was falling over and over. It felt like one of those crazy fairground rides, only he'd forgotten to buckle his seat belt. Who had designed this thing? It'd be safe enough on a calm sea but who got shipwrecked on a calm sea?

He could find nothing to anchor himself to. He was flailing, bashing against the sides of the raft with every bounce.

He felt ill but he didn't have time to be ill.

At least Jake was safe. It was a mantra, and he said it over and over. He had to believe the chopper had pulled his twin to safety. Thinking anything else was the way of madness.

The raft crashed again, but this time it was different. It was smashing against something solid.

They'd been miles from land when the yacht had started taking on water. Ben knew what this must be and his nausea increased. The raft would be bashing against what remained of the yacht's hull. Caught in the same currents, with no way to get himself clear, he'd be hurled against timber at every turn.

The second crash ripped the side of the life raft. Another wave hurled over him, and the life raft practically turned itself inside out.

Tossing its human cargo out with it.

He grabbed one of the ropes around the outside of the raft. The bulk of the craft should stay upright. If he could just hold…

Another wave hit, a massive breaker of surging foam. No man could hold against such force.

And then there was nothing. Only the open, smashing sea. The GPS was in the life raft. Chances of being found now? Zip.

It was no use swimming. There was no use doing anything but hope his lifejacket wouldn't be torn from him. He could only hope he could still keep on breathing. Hope… Hope…

There was nothing but hope. He was fighting to breathe. He was fighting to live.

There was no help. There was nothing but the endless sea.

She had to round the headland to get to the cave. It meant putting her head down and pulling almost directly into the wind. She had no idea how she was doing it, but the trolley was moving.

Tourists came to this place in summer, beaching their kayaks and exploring. The cliff path had therefore been trodden almost flat. It was possible, and she had terror driving her on. 'This is mad,' she muttered, but her words were lost in the gale.

She was at the point where the path veered away from the headland and turned towards the safety of the cave. Five more steps. Four…

She reached the turn and glanced down towards the beach,

beyond the headland where the storm was at its worst. And stopped.

Was that a figure in the water, just beyond the shallows? A body? A crimson lifejacket?

She was surely imagining things, but, dear God, if she wasn't…

Triage. Her medical training kicked in. Get the provisions safe, she told herself. She was no use to herself or anyone else without dry gear.

She had to haul the trolley upwards for the last few yards but she hardly noticed. In seconds she'd shoved the trolley deep inside the cave. At least the cave was in the lee of the storm, and so was the beach below.

It was wild enough even on the safe side of the island.

'Stay,' she told Heinz, and Heinz stuck his head out from the plastic bags and promptly buried himself again. Stay? He was in total agreement. It was dry and safe in the cave but outside the scream of wind and ocean was terrifying.

She had to face it. She wasn't sure what she'd seen was… someone, but she had to find out.

The path down to the beach was steep but manageable. Running along the beach on the lee side of the island was almost easy as well. Thankfully the tide was out so she was running on wet sand.

She could do this.

And then she rounded the headland and the force of the storm hit head on.

She could hardly see. Wind and sand were blasting her face, blinding her.

Was it all her imagination? Was she risking herself for a bit of floating debris? The tide was coming in—fast.

She'd come this far. There were rocks at the water's edge. She was pushing her way along the rocks, frantically searching, trying to see out into the waves. Where…?

He was falling and falling and falling. He had no idea how long he'd been in the water, how far he'd drifted, how desperate his position was. All he knew was that every few seconds he had to find the will to breathe. It was as easy and as impossible as that.

His body was no longer his own. The sea was doing what it willed. Waves were crashing over and around him. The chance to breathe often stretched to twenty, even thirty seconds.

He could think of nothing but breathing.

But then something sharp was crashing against his leg. And then his shoulder. Something hard, immoveable…

Solid. Rocks?

The water washed out and for a blessed moment he felt himself free of the water.

Another wave and it must have been twenty seconds before he could breathe. Whatever he was lying on seemed to be holding him down.

Another wash of water and he was free, hurled away from the sharpness, tossed high.

Onto sand?

He was barely conscious but he got it. His face was buried in sand.

Until the next wave.

Somehow he lifted his head. Sand. Rocks. Cliff.

The water came again but he was ready for it. He dug down, clung like a limpet.

The wave swept out again and somehow miraculously he stayed.

He couldn't resist the water's force again, though. He had to crawl out of the reach of the waves' power. Somehow…somehow… The world was an aching, hurting blur. The sand was the only thing he could cling to.

He clung and clung.

And through it all was the mantra. Make Jake safe. Dear God, make Jake be okay.

Another wave. Somehow he managed to claw himself higher, but at what cost? The pain in his leg…in his head…

He could close his eyes, he thought. Just for a moment.

If Jake was safe he could close his eyes and forget.

* * *

And then she found it. Him.

Dear God, this was no detritus washed up in the storm. This was a dark-haired, strongly built man, wearing yachting gear and a lifejacket.

He was face down in the sand. He'd lost a shoe. His pants were ripped. Lifeless?

As she reached him she could see a thin line of blood seeping down his face. Fresh blood. He'd been alive when he'd been washed up.

His hands were sprawled out on the sand. She knelt and touched one and flinched with the cold. His skin was white and clammy—how long had he been in the water?

She touched his neck.

A pulse! Alive!

She hauled him over—no mean feat by itself—so he lay on his side rather than face down. She was frantically trying to clear sand from mouth and nostrils. She had her ear against his mouth.

He was breathing. She could hear it. She unclipped his lifejacket and she could see the faint rise and fall of his chest.

There was so much sand. His face was impossibly caked. Wiping was never going to get rid of that sand.

He'd be sucking it into his lungs.

She hauled off her raincoat and headed into the waves, stooping to scoop water into the plastic. That was a risk by itself because the waves were fierce. She backed up fast, up the beach to where he lay, then placed her back to the wind and oozed the water carefully around his face. She was trying to rid him of the caked sand. How much had he already breathed?

Why was he unconscious? That hit on the head? Near drowning? With his mouth clear, she put her mouth against his and breathed for him. It wouldn't hurt to help him, to get more oxygen in, to keep that raspy breathing going.

His chest rose and fell, rose and fell, more surely now that she was breathing with him.

She kept on breathing while the sleet slashed from all sides, while the wind howled and while wet sand cut into her face and hands, every part of her that was exposed.

What to do? The tide was coming in. In an hour, probably less, this beach would be under water.

She thought of the trolley, but to pull it on a sandy beach was impossible. This man must be six foot three or four and strongly built. She was five foot six and no wimp, but she was no match for this guy's size.

How to move him? She couldn't.

'Please,' she pleaded out loud, and she didn't even know what she was pleading for.

But as if he'd heard, his body shifted. He opened his eyes and stared up at her.

Deep, grey eyes. Wounded eyes. She'd seen pain before and this man had it in spades.

'You're safe,' she said, keeping her voice low and calm. Nurse reassuring patient. Nurse telling lies? 'You're okay. Relax.'

'Jake...' he muttered.

'Is that your name?'

'No, Ben. But Jake...'

'I'm Mary and we can worry about Jake when we're off the beach,' she said, still in the reassuring tone she'd honed with years of district nursing. 'I'm here to help. Ben, the tide's coming in and we need to move. Can you wiggle your toes?'

She could see him think about it. Concentrate.

His feet moved. Praise be. She wasn't coping with paraplegia—or worse.

She should be factoring in risks. She should have him on a rigid board with a neck brace in case of spinal injury.

There wasn't time. Survival meant they had to move.

'Now your legs,' she said, and one leg moved. The other shifted a little and then didn't. She could see pain wash over his face.

'That's great,' she said, even though it wasn't. 'We have one good leg and one that's sore. Now fingers and arms.'

'I can't feel 'em.'

'That's because you're cold. Try.'

He tried and they moved.

'Good. Take a breather now. We have a little time.' Like five minutes. Waves were already reaching his feet.

He had a slash across his face. The bleeding had slowed to an ooze but it looked like it had bled profusely.

Head injury. He needed X-rays. If he had intracranial bleeding...

Don't even go there.

Priorities. She had a patient with an injured leg and blood loss and shock. The tide was coming in. There was time for nothing but getting him off the beach.

The sand and sleet were slapping her face, making her gasp. She was having trouble breathing herself.

Think.

Injured leg. She had no time—or sight—to assess it. The slashing sand was blinding.

Splint.

Walking-stick.

She made to rise but his hand came out and caught her. He held her arm, with surprising strength.

'Don't leave me.' It was a gasp.

She understood. She looked at the ripped lifejacket and then she looked out at the mountainous sea.

This guy must be one of the yachties they'd been talking about on the radio this morning. A yacht race—the Ultraswift Round the World Challenge—had been caught unprepared. The cyclone warning had had the fleet running for cover to Auckland but the storm had veered unexpectedly, catching them in its midst.

At dawn the broadcasters had already been talking about capsizes and deaths. Heroic rescues. Tragedy.

Now the storm had turned towards her island. It must have swept Ben before it. He'd somehow been swept onto Hideaway, but to safety?

Would this be as bad as the storm got, or would the cyclone

hit them square on? With no radio contact she had to assume the worst.

She had to get him off this beach.

'I'm not leaving you,' she said, and heaven only knew the effort it cost to keep the panic from her voice. 'I'm walking up the beach to find you a walking-stick. Then I'm coming back to help you to safety. I know you can't see me clearly right now but I'm five feet six inches tall and even though I play roller derby like a champion, I can't carry you. You need a stick.'

'Roller derby,' he said faintly.

'My team name is Smash 'em Mary,' she said. 'You don't want to mess with me.'

'Smash 'em Mary?' It was a ragged whisper but she was satisfied. She'd done what she'd intended. She'd made him think of something apart from drama and tragedy.

'I'll invite you to a game some time,' she told him. 'But not today. Bite on a bullet, big boy, while I fetch you a walking-stick.'

'I don't need a walking-stick.'

'Yeah, you can get up and hike right up the beach without even a wince,' she said. 'I don't think so. Lie still and think of nothing at all while I go and find what I need. Do what the lady tells you. Stay.'

Stay. He had no choice.

'Smash 'em Mary.' The name echoed in his head, weirdly reassuring.

The last few hours had been a nightmare. In the end he'd decided it was a dream. He'd been drifting in and out of consciousness or that was how it'd seemed. The past was mixing with the future. He and Jake as kids in that great, ostentatious mansion their parents called home. Their father yelling at them. 'You moronic imbeciles, you're your mother's spawn. You've inherited nothing from me. Stupid, stupid, stupid.'

That's how he felt now. Stupid.

Jake, flying through the air with the blast from the roadside bomb. Stupid, stupid, stupid.

Jake on a rope, smashing through the waves.

'Ben, look after your brother.' That was their mother. Rita Marlene. Beautiful, fragile, fatally flawed. 'Promise me.'

She was here now. *Promise me.*

Where was Jake?

This was all a dream.

His mother?

Smash 'em Mary.

There was no way a dream could conjure a Smash 'em Mary. The name hauled him out of his stupor as nothing else could.

Stay.

He had no choice but to obey. The nightmare was still there. If he moved, it might slam back.

He'd lie still and submit. To Smash 'em Mary?

She'd been so close he'd seen her face. She had an elfin haircut, with wet, short-cropped curls plastering her forehead. She had a finely boned face, brown eyes and freckles.

She had shadows under her eyes. Exhaustion?

Because of him? Had she been searching for him—or someone else?

How many yachts had gone down?

Memory was surging back, and he groaned and tried to rise. But then she was back, pushing him down onto the sand.

'Disobedience means no elephant stamp,' she told him. 'I said lie still and I meant lie still.' Then she faltered a little, and the assurance faded. 'Ben, I can't sugar-coat this. Your leg might be broken and there's no way I can assess it here.

'In normal circumstances I'd call an ambulance, we'd fill you full of nice woozy drugs, put you on a stretcher and cart you off to a hospital, but right now all you have is me. So I've found a couple of decent sticks. I'll tie one to your leg to keep it still. The other's a walking-stick. You're going to hold onto me and we'll get you off this beach.'

He tried to think about it. It was hard to think about anything but closing his eyes and going to sleep.

'Ben,' Mary snapped. 'Don't even think about closing your eyes. You're cold to the marrow. The tide's coming in. You go to sleep and you won't wake up.'

'What's wrong with that?' It was a slur. It was so hard to make his voice work.

'Because Jake needs you,' Mary snapped again. 'You pull yourself together and help me, and then we'll both help Jake. Just do it.'

And put like that, of course he'd do it. He had no choice.

Afterwards she could never figure out how they managed. She'd read somewhere of mothers lifting cars off children, superhuman feats made possible by the adrenalin of terror. There was something about a cyclone bearing down that provided the same sort of impetus.

She was facing sleet and sand and the blasting of leaves and branches from the storm-swept trees of Hideaway Island and beyond. She had to get this man two hundred yards up a rocky cliff to the safety of the cave. The sheer effort of hauling him was making her feel faint, but there was no way she was letting him go.

'If I had to find a drowned rat of a sailor, why couldn't I have found a little one?' she gasped. They were halfway up the path, seemingly a million miles from the top. Ben was grim-faced with pain. He was leaning on his stick but his left leg was useless and he was forced to lean on her heavily. His weight was almost unbearable.

'Leave me and come back when the storm's done,' he gasped.

'No way,' she said, and then, as he propped himself up on the walking-stick, turning stubborn, she hauled out the big guns. 'Keep going. Jake needs you even if I don't.' She didn't have a clue who Jake was but it shut him up. He went back to concentrating on one ghastly step at a time, and so did she.

His leg seemed useless. He was totally dependent on one leg, his stick and her support. Compound fracture? Blocked blood supply? There hadn't been the time or visibility on the beach to see. She'd simply ripped her coat into strips and tied the stick on his leg to keep it as steady as she could.

But it was bad. He was dragging it behind him and she could feel that every step took him to the edge.

She felt close to the edge herself. How much worse must it be for him?

'If I were you, I'd be screaming in agony,' she managed, and she felt him stiffen. She could feel his tension, his fear—and now his shock.

'Smash…Smash 'em Mary screams in agony?'

'I'm good at it,' she confessed. 'It's great for getting free points from the referee.'

'You're…kidding me.'

'Nope.' She was trying desperately to sound normal, to keep the exhaustion from her voice as they hauled themselves one appalling step after another. Dizziness was washing over her in waves, but she wouldn't succumb. 'I've watched wrestlers on the telly. I swear their agony is pretend but they make millions. Some day I might.'

'As a wrestler, or with roller derby?'

'I might need to work on my muscles a bit for wrestling. I should have done it earlier. Muscles'd be helping now.'

They surely would. He was doing his best but she was practically dragging him.

Left to his own devices, he'd have lain where he was until the storm passed. Or not. This diminutive woman was giving him no choice.

'Mary—'

'Shut up and keep going.'

'You don't have to—'

'Lie down and we lie down together,' she muttered, grim with determination. 'I don't give up. I might get it horribly wrong, but I don't give up. Ever.'

He had no clue what that meant. All he knew was that she

was iron. She wasn't faltering. No matter how steep the ground grew, she wasn't slowing.

But she stopped talking. She must be as close to the edge as he was, he thought. If he could only help...

And then suddenly, blessedly, the ground flattened. His leg jolted with the shock of a change of levels but she didn't pause.

'Heinz... Heinz's waiting just round this corner.' She was gasping for breath, not bothering to disguise her distress now they were on level ground.

'Heinz?'

'My...my guard dog.'

Somehow she hauled him another few steps, around a bluff that instantly, magically chopped off the screaming wind. Ten more steps took them towards darkness...the mouth of a cave? Five more steps and they were inside. The rain ceased. The light dimmed.

'Welcome to my lair,' Mary managed, and that was all she could get out.

'I can't...' she muttered—and she folded into a crumpled heap.

What the...?

Somehow he dropped beside her, fumbling to lift her head, to clear her face from the sandy ground. Was this a faint? Please, God, let this just be exhaustion. To have hauled him so far...

This woman had put her own life on the line to save his. She'd given her all and more. Her faint had to be from sheer exhaustion, he told himself fiercely. It had to be. If it was worse, he'd carry the guilt for the rest of his life.

Her eyes were open, dazed, confused.

'Hey,' he managed. 'It's okay. We're safe now. You've saved me, now it's your turn to relax.'

He was so close to the edge himself. He could do so little but he did his best. Somehow he got his arm under her shoulders. He lifted her head so her face was resting on his chest instead of the rock and sand. He felt her heartbeat against his.

Somehow he hauled her deeper into the cave, tugging her

along with him. His leg jabbed like a red-hot poker smashing down.

They were out of the wind. They were out of danger.

He held her but he could do no more. The darkness was closing in. The pain in his leg... He couldn't think past it.

Exhaustion held sway. He closed his eyes and the dim light became dark.

CHAPTER TWO

SOMETHING WARM AND rough was washing his face.

Someone was hauling away his clothes.

How long had he let darkness enfold him? Too long, it seemed. Things were happening that were out of his control.

Who was he kidding? He'd been out of control ever since the yacht's mast had snapped. Or ever since the cyclone had turned and headed straight for them.

His sodden jacket and sweater were off. There was a towel around his chest.

His pants were coming off. He grabbed at them but too late—they were down past his knees and further.

The face washer was working faster.

'Heinz, leave the man alone. He's all sandy,' a voice said. 'He'll taste disgusting.'

His rescuing angel was alive and bossy again, and for a moment relief threatened to overwhelm him. She'd survived. They both had.

He opened his eyes. There was a light to his left, a flame, a crackling of wood catching fire.

A dog was between him and the flame. A scruffy-looking terrier-type dog, knee-high, tongue dangling for future use and his tail waving hopefully, like adventure was just around the corner.

His pants disappeared. He had what seemed like a towel around his torso. Nothing else?

A blanket was lowered over his chest on top of the towel. Fuzzy. Dry. Bliss!

Not over his legs.

'Now let's see the damage.' The bossy, prosaic voice was becoming almost a part of him. He wanted to hold on to that voice. It seemed all that stood between him and the abyss. 'But first let me wriggle a blanket under you. I need to get you warm.'

Two hands held him, hip and chest. They rolled, slowly but firmly, just enough to haul him on his side. His leg responded with even more pain, but her body held him close enough to her to stop his leg flopping. The rolled blanket slipped under, unrolling so he had a base that wasn't sand. Her hands rolled him the other way and he was on a makeshift bed.

It had been a professional move.

She was a roller-derbying medic?

'Who...who are you?'

'I told you. Mary to my friends. Smash 'em Mary to those who get in my way.' She hauled something else over the top of him, some kind of quilt. Soft and deep.

He was naked? How had that happened?

He wasn't asking questions. The blanket was under him. The quilt was on top. The beginnings of warmth...

If it wasn't for his leg he could give in to it but his leg was reminding him of damage with one vicious jolt after another. The fearsome throbbing left room for little else, pushing him back to the abyss.

She had a torch and was playing its beam down on the source of pain. He felt light fingers touching, not adding to the pain, just feather-light exploring.

'I want an X-ray,' she said fretfully.

'I'd assumed you'd have the equipment,' he managed, trying desperately to get his words to sound normal. 'X-ray equipment in the next room.' What else did she have in this cave? That he was lying on a blanket under a quilt with a fire beside him was amazing all by itself. The pain eased off for a moment but then...

Jake.

Jake was suddenly front and centre, his body dangling precariously from the chopper.

'Who's Jake?' she asked. Had he said his name aloud? Who knew? His head was doing strange things. His body was no longer under his control.

'My...my brother,' he managed. Hell, Jake... 'My twin.'

'I'm guessing he was on the boat with you.'

'Yes.'

'Idiots,' she said, bitterly. 'Off you go, great macho men, pitting yourselves against the elements, leaving your womenfolk lighting candles against your return.' She was still examining his leg. 'I remember my dad singing that song, *"Men must work and women must weep...and the harbour bar be moaning..."* I bet you didn't even have to work. I bet you did it just to prove you're he-men.'

It was so close to the truth he couldn't answer. He and Jake, pushing the boundaries for as long as he could remember.

'No...no womenfolk,' he managed.

'Except me,' she said bitterly. 'Lucky me. Was Jake with you? Could he be down on the beach as well?'

And he knew, he just knew that, no matter how warm and safe this refuge was, if he said yes she'd be out there again, scouring the beach for drowned sailors. She'd passed out from exhaustion and yet she was ready to go again. This wasn't a woman for weeping. This was a woman for doing.

'No,' he managed.

'You got separated?'

'We were well clear of the rest of the fleet, making a run for the Bay of Islands.'

'Which is where you are.'

'Great,' he managed. 'But I hadn't planned on floating the last few miles.'

'And Jake?'

'They tried to take him off.' He was having real trouble getting his voice to work. 'The last run of the rescue chopper.'

'Tried?'

'They lowered a woman with a harness. The last I saw he was hanging on to the rescue rope off the chopper.'

'Was he in the harness?'

'Y-yes.' Hell, it was hard to think. 'They both were.'

'Well, there you go, then,' she said, in such a prosaic way that it broke through his terror. 'So the last time you saw him he was being raised into a rescue chopper. I know those teams. They never lose their man. They'll bring him all the way to Auckland dangling from his harness if they have to, and he'll get the best view of the storm of anyone in the country. So now I can stop fretting about idiot Jake and focus on idiot Ben. Ben, I reckon your kneecap is dislocated, not broken.'

'Dislocated?' What did it matter? Broken, dislocated, if he had his druthers he'd have it removed. But there was an over-riding shift in the lead around his heart. Jake was safe? What was it about her words that had him believing her?

But she was now focused on his leg. 'You've figured I'm a nurse?' she demanded. 'I spent two years in an orthopaedic ward and I think I recognise this injury. Given normal circumstances, I wouldn't touch this with a barge pole. If it's broken then I stand to do more damage. But we're on the edge of a cyclone. The island you've been washed up on is the smallest and farthest out of the group and I have no radio reception. There's no way we can get help, maybe for a couple of days. If I leave this much longer you might be facing permanent disability. So how do you feel about me trying to put it back?'

He didn't feel anything but his leg.

'Ben, I'm asking for a bit more of that he-man courage,' she said, her voice gentling. 'Will you trust me to do this?'

Did he trust her?

His world was fuzzy with pain. He'd spent hours with the sea tossing him where it willed. He'd convinced himself Jake was dead.

Right now this sprite had hauled him from the sea, almost killing herself in the process. She'd put him on something soft. She'd given him Jake back. Now she was offering to fix…

'It'll hurt more while I'm doing it,' she said, and he thought, Okay, possibly not fix.

'And if it's broken I might do more damage—but, honestly, Ben, it does look dislocated.'

And he heard her worry. For the first time he heard her fear.

She was making a call, he thought, but she wasn't sure. If his leg was broken, she could hurt him more.

But her instincts said fix, and right now all he had in the world were her instincts.

'Go for it.'

'You won't sue if you end up walking backwards?'

'I'll think of you every time I do.'

She choked on laughter that sounded almost hysterical. Then she took a deep breath and he felt her settle.

'Okay. I'm going to wedge pillows behind you so you're half sitting and your hip is bent. That should loosen the quadriceps holding everything tight. Then I'm going to slowly straighten your knee, applying gentle pressure to the side of the kneecap until I can tease it back into place. I can't do it fast, because force could make any broken bone worse, so you'll just have to grit anything you have to grit while I work. Can you do that, Ben?'

'If you can, I can,' he said simply. 'Do it.'

To say it was an uncomfortable few minutes was putting it mildly. There was nothing mild about what happened next. When finally Mary grunted in satisfaction he felt sick.

'Don't you dare vomit in my nice clean cave,' she said, and her tremor revealed the strain he'd put her through. She was tucking the great soft quilt around him again. 'Not now it's over. I've done it, Ben. You can relax. If you promise not to vomit, I'll give you some water.'

'Whisky?'

'And don't we both need that? Sorry, my cellar doesn't run to fancy. Water it is.'

She held a bottle to his lips, and he hadn't realised how thirsty he was. How much salt water had he swallowed?

He tried a grunt of thanks that didn't quite come off.

'Stop now,' he managed. 'Rest…rest yourself.'

He couldn't say anything else. The blackness was waiting to receive him.

Rest? She'd love to but she daren't. She was back in control.

What had she been about, fainting? She'd never done such a thing. Probably if she had no one would have noticed, she conceded, but now, regaining consciousness sprawled on this man's chest had scared her almost into fainting again.

She had no intention of doing so. She was in control now, as she always was. To lose control was terrifying.

So she hauled herself back into efficiency. She cleaned his face, noting the blood had come from a jagged scratch from his hairline to behind his ear. Not too deep. She washed it and applied antiseptic and he didn't stir.

He looked tough, she thought. Weathered. A true sailor? There were lines around his eyes that looked wrong. What was he, thirty-five or so? Those lines said he was older. Those lines said life had been tough.

Who was he?

What was she supposed to do with him?

Nothing. Outside the wind was doing crazy things. The way the cave was facing, the sleet with the wind behind it seemed almost a veranda by itself. The ground swept down and away, which meant they were never going to be wet.

So now it was like being in front of a television, with the entrance to the cave showing terror. Trees had been slashed over, bent almost double. The sea through the rain was a churning maelstrom.

They'd only just made it in time, she thought. If this guy was still on the beach now…

She shuddered and she couldn't stop. She was so very cold. Her raincoat was in tatters and she was soaked.

Heinz whined and crept close. She hugged him.

Control, she told herself. Keep a hold of yourself.

The wind outside was screaming.

She stoked up the fire with as much wood as she dared. There was driftwood at the cave entrance—she should drag more inside, but she didn't want to go near that wind.

She couldn't stop the tremors.

'Rest yourself,' he'd said, and the urge to do so was suddenly urgent.

Ben was lying on her blanket. He was covered by her friend's gorgeous quilt. Queen-sized.

He looked deeply asleep. Exhausted.

She might just accept that she was exhausted as well.

She should stay alert and keep watch.

For what? What more could she do? If the wind swung round they were in trouble, but there was nothing she could do to prevent it.

If her sailor stirred she needed to know.

She was so cold.

She touched his skin under the quilt and he was cold, too. Colder than she was, despite the quilt.

What would a sensible woman do?

What a sensible woman had to do. She hauled off her outer clothes. She left her bra and knickers on—a woman had to preserve some decency.

She arranged her wet clothes and Ben's on the trolley, using it as a clothes horse by the fire.

She hugged Heinz close and gently wriggled them both onto the blanket.

Under the quilt.

She'd hauled off Ben's soggy clothes but she winced as she felt his skin. He was so cold. How long had he been in the water?

There should be procedures for this sort of situation. Some way she could use her body to warm him without...without what? Catching something?

Catching cold. This was crazy.

'Men must work and women must weep...'

Not this woman. This woman put her arms around her frigid

sailor, curled her body so as much skin as possible was touching, tried not to think she was taking as much comfort as she was giving...

And tried to sleep.

CHAPTER THREE

HE WOKE AND he was warm.

How cold had he been and for how long? There was a nightmare somewhere in the dark, the pain in his leg, his terror for Jake. They were waiting to enclose him again, but the nightmare was all about cold and noise and motion, and right now he was enclosed in a cloud of warmth and softness, and he was holding a woman.

Or she was holding him. He was on his back, his head on cushions. She was curved by his side, lying on her front, her head in the crook of his shoulder, her arm over his chest, as if she would cover as much of his body as she could.

Which was fine by him. The warmth and the comfort of skin against skin was unbelievable.

There was a bit of fur there as well. A dog? On the other side of him.

Well, why wouldn't there be, for on that side was a fire.

He was enfolded by dog and woman and hearth.

Words came back to him…

'Men must work and women must weep'?

Had she said that to him, this woman? Some time in the past?

This woman wasn't weeping. This woman was all about giving herself to him, feeding him warmth, feeding him safety.

He didn't move. Why move? He remembered a wall of pain and he wasn't going there. If he shifted an inch, it might return.

Who was she, this woman? She was soundly asleep, her body

folded against his. Some time during the darkness he must have moved to hold her. One of his arms held her loosely against him.

Mine.

It was a thought as primeval as time itself. Claiming a woman.

Claiming a need.

His body was responding.

Um…not. Not even in your dreams, he told himself, but the instinctive stirring brought reality back. Or as much reality as he could remember.

The yacht, the *Rita Marlene*.

The storm.

Jake, hanging from that rope.

'Want to tell me about it?'

Her voice was slurred with sleep. She didn't move. She didn't pull away. This position, it seemed, was working for them both.

It was the deepest of intimacies and he knew nothing about her. Nothing except she'd saved his life.

She must have felt him stiffen. Something had woken her but she wasn't pulling away. She seemed totally relaxed, part of the dark.

Outside he could still hear the screaming of the storm. Here there was only them.

'You already told me I'm a dumb male. What else is there to tell?'

He felt her smile. How could he do that? How did he feel like he knew this woman?

Something about skin against skin?

Something about her raw courage?

'There's variations of dumb,' she said. 'So you were in the yacht race.'

'We were.'

'You and Jake-on-the-Rope.'

'Yep.' There was even reassurance there, too. She'd said Jake-on-the-Rope like it was completely normal that his brother should be swinging on a rope from a chopper somewhere out over the Southern Ocean.

'You're from the States.'

'A woman of intuition.'

'Not dumb at all. How many on the boat?'

'Two.'

'So you're both rescued,' she said with satisfaction, and he settled even further. Pain was edging back now. Actually, it was quite severe pain. His leg throbbed. His head hurt. Lots of him hurt.

It was as if once he was reassured about Jake he could feel something else.

Actually, he could feel a lot else. He could feel this woman. He could feel this woman in the most intimate way in the world.

'So tell me about the boat?' she asked.

'Rita Marlene.'

'Pretty name.'

'After my mother.'

'She's pretty?'

'She was.'

'Was,' she said. 'Sorry.'

'A long time ago now.' This was almost dream-speaking, he thought. Not real. Dark. Warm. Hauled from death. Nothing mattered but the warmth and this woman draped over him.

'You sailed all the way from the States?'

'It's an around-the-world challenge, only we were stopping here. Jake's an actor. He's due to start work on a set in Auckland.'

'Would I have heard of…Jake?'

'Jake Logan.'

'Ooh, I have.' The words were excited but not the tone. The tone was sleepy, part of the dream. 'He was in *Stitch in Time,* and *ER.* A sexy French surgeon. So not French?'

'No.'

'My stepsister will be gutted. He's her favourite Hollywood hunk.'

'Not yours?'

'I have enough to worry about without pretend heroes.'

'Like antiheroes washed up on your beach?'

'You said it.' But he heard her smile.

There was silence for a while. The fire was dying down. The pain in his knee was growing worse, but he didn't want to move from this comfort and it seemed neither did she.

But finally she did, sighing and stirring, and as her body slid from his he felt an almost gut-wrenching sense of loss.

His Mary...

His Mary? What sort of concept was that? A crazy one?

She slipped from under the quilt and shifted around to the fire. He could see her then, a faint, lit outline.

Slight. Short, cropped curls. Finely boned, her face a little like Audrey Hepburn's.

She was wearing only knickers and bra, slivers of lace that hid hardly anything.

His Mary?

Get over it.

'Heinz, you're blocking the heat from our guest,' she said reprovingly, but the dog didn't stir.

'I'm warm.'

'Thanks to Barbara's quilt,' she said. 'Her great-grandmother made that quilt. It's been used as a wall hanging for a hundred years. If we've wrecked it we're dead meat.'

He thought about it. He'd more than likely bled on it. No matter. He held it a little tighter.

'I'll give her a million for it.'

'A million!'

'Two.'

'Right,' she said dryly. 'So you're a famous actor, too?'

'A financier.'

'Someone who makes serious money?'

'Maybe.'

'You mean Heinz and I could hold you for ransom?'

'You could hold me any way you want.'

Um…no. Wrong thing to say. This might be a dream-like situation but reality got a toehold fast.

'I'm sure I told you my rollerball name,' she said, quite lightly. 'Smash 'em Mary. Some things aren't worth thinking about.'

She was five foot five or five foot six. He was six four. Ex-commando.

He smiled.

'Laugh all you want, big boy,' she said. 'But I hold the pain-killers. Speaking of which, do you want some?'

'Painkillers,' he said, and he couldn't get the edge out of his voice fast enough.

'Bad, huh?' She'd loaded wood onto the fire, and now she turned back to him, lifted Heinz away—much to the little dog's disgust—and checked his face. She put her hand on his neck and felt his pulse, and then tucked the quilt tighter.

'What hurts most?

There was a question. He must have hit rocks, he thought, but, then, he'd been hurled about the lifeboat a few times, too.

'Leg mostly,' he managed. 'Head a bit.'

'Could I ask you not to do any internal bleeding?' She flicked on her torch and examined his head, running her fingers care-fully through his hair. The hair must be stiff with salt and blood, and her fingers had a job getting through.

Hell, his body was responding again…

'Bumps and scrapes but nothing seemingly major apart from the scratch on your face,' she said. 'But I would like an X-ray.'

'There's no ferry due to take us to the mainland?'

'You reckon a ferry would run in this?' She gestured to the almost surreal vision of storm against the mouth of the cave. 'I do have a boat,' she said. 'Sadly it's moored in a natural harbour on the east of the island. East. That would be where you came from. Where the storm comes from. Any minute I'm expect-ing my boat to fly past the cave on its way to Australia. But, Ben, I do have codeine tablets. Are you allergic to anything?'

'You really are a nurse?'

'I was. Luckily for you, no one's taken my bag off me yet. Allergies?'

'No.'

'Codeine it is, then, plus an antinauseant. I don't fancy scrubbing this cave. You want to use the bathroom?'

'No!'

'It's possible,' she said, and once again he fancied he could feel her grinning behind the torch beam. 'The ledge outside the cave is sheltered and there's bushland in the lee of the cliff. I could help.'

'I'll thank you, no.'

'You want an en suite? A nice fancy flush or nothing?'

'Lady, I've been in Afghanistan,' he said, goaded, before he could stop himself.

'As a soldier?'

'Yes.' No point lying.

'That explains your face,' she said prosaically. 'And the toughness. Thank God for Afghanistan. I'm thinking it may well have saved your life. But even if we don't have an en suite, you can forget tough here, Ben. Not when I'm looking after you. Just take my nice little pills and settle down again. Let the pain go away.'

Her clothes were dry on one side and not the other. She rearranged them, wrapped a towel around herself and headed out to the ledge to look out over the island.

If there wasn't an overhang on the cliff she wouldn't be out here. The flying debris was terrifying.

It was almost dark, but in truth it had been almost dark for the last few hours. She checked her watch—it had been four hours since she'd hauled her soldier/sailor/financier up here.

The storm was getting worse.

She had so much to think about but for some reason she found herself thinking of the unknown Jake. Twin to Ben.

She only had a hazy recollection of the shows he'd been on, but she did know who he was. One of her stepsisters had raved about how sexy Jake Logan was. Mary remembered because it had been yet another appalling night of family infighting. Her stepsister had been trying to make her boyfriend jealous and he'd been rising to the bait. Her stepmother had been taking her sister's side. Her father had, as usual, been saying nothing.

She'd only arrived because she'd tried one last-ditch time to say how sorry she was. To make things right.

It had been useless. Her family wouldn't interrupt their fighting to listen. It was her fault.

Her fault, her fault, her fault.

Terrific. She was surrounded by a cyclone, she had a badly injured guy stuck in her cave—and she was dwelling on past nightmares.

Think of current nightmares.

Think of Jake.

She'd given some fast reassurance to Ben, but, in truth, the last radio report she'd heard before communications had been cut had been appalling. The cyclone had decimated the yachting fleet, and the reporter she'd heard had been talking of multiple deaths.

There'd been an interview with the head of the chopper service and he'd been choked with emotion.

'The last guy…we came so close… We thought we had him but, hell, the wind… It just slammed everything. The whole crew's gutted.'

The last guy…

Was that Ben's Jake?

She had no way of knowing, and there was no way she was passing on such a gut-wrenching supposition to Ben.

She felt…useless.

'But I did save him,' she told herself, and Heinz nosed out to see what was going on; whether it might be safe enough for a dog to find a tree.

Not. A gust blasted across the cliff in front of them; he whimpered and backed inside.

'You and Ben,' Mary muttered. 'Wussy males.'

She glanced back into the cave. All was dark. All was well.

She hoped. She still had no way of telling whether Ben's leg was fractured or, worse, if that crack on his head had been severe enough to cause subdural haemorrhaging. What if she walked back in and he was dead?

She walked back in and he was asleep, breathing deeply and evenly, with Heinz nuzzling back down against him.

What to do?

What was there to do? Sit by the fire and imagine subdural bleeding or twins falling from ropes into a cyclone-ravaged sea? Think of home, her family, the past that had driven her here?

Or do what she'd been doing for the last few weeks?

She lit a fat candle. Between it and the fire she could sort of see.

She shoved a couple of cushions behind her, she tucked a blanket over her legs, she put her manuscript on her knees and she started to write.

The door to the bar swung open.

She glanced at the sleeping guy not six feet from her.

He was six foot three or four, lean, mean, dangerous. His deep grey eyes raked every corner of the room.
Could he tell she was a werewolf?

She grinned. Hero or villain? She hadn't figured which but it didn't matter. There was a nice meaty murder about to happen in the room upstairs. A little blood was about to drip on people's heads. Maybe a lot of blood. She wasn't sure where Ben Logan would fit but he'd surely add drama.

'Call me Logan,' he drawled...

She thought maybe she'd have to do a search and replace when she reached the end. Maybe calling a character after her wounded sailor wasn't such a good idea.

But for now it helped. For now her villain/hero Logan could keep the storm at bay.

There was nothing like a bit of fantasy when a woman needed it most.

He woke, and she was heating something on the fire.

That's what had woken him, he thought. The smell was unbelievable. Homey, spicy, the smell of meat and herbs filled the cave.

He stirred and winced and she turned from the fire and smiled at him. Outside was black. No light was getting in now. Her face was lit by flickering firelight and one candle.

'Hey,' she said. 'Dinner?'

He thought about it for a nanosecond or less. 'Yes, please.'

'You can have the bowl. I'll use the frying pan. I wasn't anticipating guests. Would you like to sit up a little?'

'Um…'

She grinned. 'Yeah, I'm guessing what you need before food. Are you ready to admit I might be a nurse and therefore useful? If I'd known I'd have brought a bedpan.'

He sighed. 'Mary…'

'Mmm?'

'Can you hand me my clothes?'

'Knickers is all,' she said. 'The rest are still wet.' She handed him his boxers—and then had second thoughts. She tugged back the quilt and slid his boxers over his feet before he realised what she intended.

'Lift,' she ordered, and he did, and he felt about five years old.

She was still scantily dressed, too, in knickers, bra and T-shirt.

Her T-shirt was damp. He shouldn't notice.

He noticed.

'So it's okay for you to stay cold but not me?' he managed.

'That's the one.' She was helping him to stand, levering herself under his shoulder, taking his weight.

'Mary?'

'Mmm?'

'Hand me my stick. I can do this.'

'In your dreams.'

'Not in my dreams,' he said. 'For real. I won't take your help.'

'This is Smash 'em Mary you're talking to. I'm tough.'

'This is a five-feet-five-inch runt I'm talking to. Let me be.'

'You want to sign an indemnity form so if you fall down the cliff it's not my fault?'

'It's not your fault. How could it be your fault?'

'Of course it could be,' she said, and there was a sudden and unexpected note of bitterness beneath her words. 'Somehow it always is.'

He managed. He got outside and in again. He almost made it back to his makeshift bed but he had to accept help for the last couple of yards.

He felt like he'd been hit by rocks. Maybe he had been hit by rocks.

Propped up on pillows again, he was handed beef casserole. Excellent casserole.

There were worse places for a man to recuperate.

'How did you manage this?' he demanded, intrigued.

'There's a solar-powered freezer in the cabin,' she told him. 'The solar panels were one of the first victims of the storm so I packed a pile of food and brought it here. I loaded whatever was on top of the freezer so who knows what the plastic boxes hold. This time we got lucky but we might be eating bait for breakfast.'

'The storm came up fast, then?'

'The radio said storm, tie down your outdoor furniture. They didn't say cyclone, tie down your house.'

'This isn't a cyclone,' he told her. 'Or not yet. I've been in one before. This is wild but a full-scale cyclone hits with noise that's unbelievable. We're on the fringe.'

'So it's still to hit?'

'Or miss.'

'That'd be good,' she said, but he heard worry.

'Is there someone else you're scared about?' he demanded. He hadn't thought…all the worrying he'd done up until now had been about Jake.

'You,' she said. 'You need X-rays.'

'I'm tough.'

'Yeah, and you still need X-rays.'

'I promise I won't die.' He said it lightly but he somehow had the feeling that this woman was used to expecting the worst.

Well, she was a nurse.

Nurses didn't always expect the worst.

'I'd prefer that you didn't,' she said, striving to match his lightness. 'I have a pile of freezer contents that'll be fine for up to two days but then they'll decompose. If you're decomposing too, I might be forced to evacuate my cave.'

He choked. Only a nurse could make such a joke, he thought. He remembered the tough medics who'd been there in Afghanistan and he thought…Mary could be one of those.

The nurses had saved Jake's life when he'd been hit by a roadside bomb. Not the doctors, they had been too few in the field and they'd been stretched to the limit. Nurses had managed to stop the bleeding, get fluids into his brother, keep him stable until the surgeons had time to do their thing.

He kind of liked nurses.

He kind of liked this one.

He ate the casserole and drank the tea she made—he'd never tasted tea so good—and thought about her some more.

'So no one's worrying about you?' he asked, lightly, he thought, but she looked at him with a shrewdness he was starting to expect.

'I've left a note in a bottle saying where I am and who I'm with, so watch it, mate.'

He grinned. She really was…extraordinary.

'But there is no one?'

'If you're asking if I'm single, then I'm single.'

'Parents?'

That brought a shadow. She shook her head and started clearing.

She was so slight.

She was so alone.

'You want to share a bed again?' He shifted sideways so there was room under the quilt for her.

She must be cold. The temperature wasn't all that bad—this was a summer storm—but the cave was earth-cool, and the humidity meant their clothes were taking an age to dry.

She was wearing a T-shirt but he'd felt it as she'd helped him back into bed and it was clammy.

She needed to take it off. This bed was the only place to be.

She was looking doubtful.

'It'll be like we're flatmates, watching telly on the sofa,' he said, pushing the covers back.

'I forgot to bring the telly.'

'That's professional negligence if ever I heard it.' Then he frowned at the look on her face. 'What? What did I say?'

'Nothing.' Her face shuttered, but she hauled off her T-shirt and slid under the covers—as if the action might distract him.

It did distract him. A woman like this in his bed? Watching telly? Ha!

He pushed away the thought—or the sensation—and managed to push himself far enough away so there was at last an inch between their bodies.

The temptation to move closer was almost irresistible.

Resist.

'So tell me why you're here?' he asked. If she could hear the strain in his voice he couldn't help it. He was hauling his body under control and it didn't leave a lot of energy for small talk.

Mary was an inch away.

No.

'Here. Island. Why?' he said, but the look on her face stayed. Defensive.

'You. Yacht in middle of cyclone. Why?' she snapped back.

And he thought, Yeah, this lady has shadows.

'I'm distracting my brother from a failed marriage,' he told her. He didn't do personal. The Logan brothers' private life was their own business but there was something about this woman that told him anything he exposed would go no further.

Armour on his part seemed inappropriate. Somehow it was Mary who seemed wounded. She wasn't battered like he was, not beaten by rocks and sea, but in some intensely personal way she seemed just as wounded.

So he didn't do personal but they were sharing a bed in the middle of a cyclone and personal seemed the only way to go.

'So Jake needed to be distracted?' she said cautiously.

And he thought, Yep, he'd done it. He'd taken that look off her face. The look that said she was expecting to be slapped.

Smash 'em Mary? Maybe not so tough, then.

'Jake's a bit of a target,' he said. 'He came back from Afghanistan wounded, and I suspect there are nightmares. He threw himself into acting, his career took off and suddenly there were women everywhere. He found himself with a starlet with dollars in her eyes but he couldn't see it. She used him to push her career and he was left...'

'Scarred?'

'Jake doesn't do scarred.'

'How about you?' she asked. 'Do you do scarred?'

'No!'

'How did you feel when your brother was wounded?'

The question was so unexpected that it left him stranded.

The question took him back to the dust and grit of an Afghan roadside.

They hadn't even been on duty. They'd been in different battalions and the two groups had met as Ben's battalion had been redeployed. Ben hadn't seen his brother for six months.

'I know a place with fine dining,' Jake had joked. 'Practically five-star.'

Yeah, right. Jake always knew the weird and wonderful; he was always pushing the rules. Eating in the army mess didn't fit with his vision of life.

The army didn't fit with Jake's vision of life. It was a good fit for neither of them. They'd joined to get away from their father and their family notoriety, as far as they could.

Fail. *'Logan Brothers Blasted by Roadside Bomb. Heirs to Logan Fortune Airlifted Out.'* They couldn't get much more notorious than that.

'Earth to Ben?' Mary said. 'You were saying? How did you feel when Jake was injured?'

'How do you think I felt?' He didn't talk about it, he never had, but suddenly it was all around him and the need to talk was just there. 'One minute we were walking back to base on an almost deserted road, catching up on home talk. The next moment a bus full of locals pulled up. And then an explosion.'

'Oh, Ben...'

'Schoolkids,' he said, and he was there again, surrounded by terror, death, chaos. 'They targeted kids for maximum impact. Twelve kids were killed and Jake was collateral damage.'

'No wonder he has nightmares.'

'Yeah.'

'Did he lose consciousness?'

What sort of question was that? What difference did it make?

But it did make a difference. He'd thought, among all that carnage, at least Jake was unaware.

'Until we reached the field hospital, yes.'

'You were uninjured?'

'Minor stuff. Jake was between me and the bus.'

'Then I'm guessing,' she said gently, 'that your nightmares will be worse than his.'

'I'm fine.'

'He's your younger brother.'

'By twenty minutes.'

'You'll still feel responsible.'

'He's okay.' He flinched at the thought of where he might be now. Put it away, fast. 'He has to be okay. But tell me about you. Why are you here?'

And the question was neatly turned. She had nowhere to go,

he thought as he watched her face. He'd answered her questions. He'd let down his guard. Now he was demanding entry to places he instinctively knew she kept protected.

They were two of a kind, he thought, and how he knew it he couldn't guess. But they kept their secrets well.

He was asking for hers.

'I'm escaping from my family,' she said, and she was silent for a while. 'I'm escaping from my community as well.'

'As bad as that?'

'Worse,' she said. 'Baby killer, that's me.'

It was said lightly. It was said with all the pain in the world.

'You want to tell me about it?'

'No.'

'You expect me to stay in the same bed as a baby killer?'

She turned and stared and he met her gaze. Straight and true. If this woman was a baby killer he was King Kong.

He smiled and she tried to smile back. It didn't come off.

'I've exonerated you,' he told her. 'Found you innocent. Evidence? If you really were a baby killer you'd be on a more secure island. Alcatraz, for instance. Want to tell me about it?'

'No.'

'I told you mine.' He lifted the quilt so it reached her shoulders. 'If you lie back, there are cushions. Very comfy cushions. You can stare into the dark and pretend I'm your therapist.'

'I don't need a therapist.'

'Neither do I.'

'You have nightmares.'

'And you don't?' He put gentle pressure on her shoulder. She resisted for a moment. Heinz snuffled beside her. The wind raised its howl a notch.

She slumped back on the pillows and felt the fight go out of her.

'Tell Dr Ben,' Ben said.

'Doctor?'

'I'm playing psychoanalyst. I've failed the army. I'm a long way from the New York Stock Exchange. My yacht's a hundred fathoms deep. A man has to have some sort of career. Shoot.'

'Shoot?'

'What would an analyst say? So, Ms Smash 'em Mary, you're confessing to baby killing.'

And she smiled. He heard it and he almost whooped.

What was it about this woman that made it so important to make her smile?

Shoot, he'd said, and she did.

CHAPTER FOUR

She gave in.

She told him.

'Okay,' she said, and he heard weariness now, the weariness of a long, long battle. 'I've told you that I'm a district nurse?'

'Hence the drugs,' he said. 'Nice nurse.'

She smiled again, but briefly. 'I'm currently suspended from work and a bit…on the outer with my family,' she told him. She took a deep breath. 'Okay, potted history. My mum died when I was eight. She'd been ill for a year and at the end Dad was empty. It was like most of him had died, too.

'Then he met Barbie. Barbie's some kind of faith-healer and self-declared clairvoyant. She offered to channel Mum, using Ouija boards, that kind of thing, and Dad was so desperate he fell for it. But Barbie has three daughters of her own and was in a financial mess. She was blatantly after Dad's money. Dad's well off. He has financial interests in most of the businesses in Taikohe where we live, and Barbie simply moved in and took control. She got rid of every trace of my mother. She still wants to get rid of me.'

'Cinderella with the wicked stepmother?'

'She's never mistreated me. Not overtly. She just somehow stopped Dad showing interest in me. With Barbie he seemed to die even more, if that makes sense, and she derided the things I had left to cling to.'

'There are worse ways to mistreat a child than beat them,' he said softly, and she was quiet for a while, as the wind rose and the sounds of the storm escalated.

He thought she'd stopped then, and was trying to figure how to prod her to go further when she started again, all by herself.

'School was my escape,' she told him. 'I liked school and I was good at it. I liked...rules.'

'Rules make sense when you're lost,' he agreed. 'Sometimes they're the only thing to cling to.' Was that why he and Jake had joined the army? he wondered. To find some limits?

'Anyway, I studied nursing. I became Taikohe's district nurse. I now have my own cottage...'

'With a cat?' he demanded. 'Uh-oh. This is starting to sound like cat territory.'

And she got it. He heard her grin. 'Only Heinz, who'll eat me when I die a spinster, alone and unloved.' She poked him— hard, in the ribs.

'Ow!'

'Serves you right. Of all the stereotyping males...'

'Hey, you're the one with the wicked stepmother.'

'Do you want to hear this or not?'

'Yes,' he said promptly, because he did. 'Tell Dr Ben.'

'Your bedside manner needs improving.'

'My bedside manner is perfect,' he said, and put his arm around her shoulders and tugged her closer. 'I'd like some springs in this mattress but otherwise I can't think of a single improvement.'

'Ben...'

'Go on,' he said encouragingly. 'Tell me what happened next. Tell me about the baby.'

There was a long silence. She lay still. Seemingly unbidden, his fingers traced a pattern in her hair. It felt...right to do so. Half of him expected her to pull away, but she didn't.

Tell me, he willed her silently, and wondered why it seemed so important that she did.

Finally it came.

'So now I'm grown up, living in the same community as my stepmother and my stepsisters and my dad. My dad's still like a dried-up husk. The others ignore me. I'm the dreary local nurse who uses traditional medicine, which they despise. They put up with me when I drop in to visit my dad but that's as far as the relationship goes.

'But now they've started having babies—not my stepmum but the girls. Sapphire, Rainbow and Sunrise. Home births all. No hospitals or traditional medicine need apply. They've had six healthy babies between them, with my stepmother crowing that traditional medicine's responsible for all the evils of the world. And then...catastrophe.'

'Catastrophe?'

'One dead baby,' she said, drearily now. 'Sunrise, my youngest stepsister, is massively overweight. The pregnancy went two weeks over term but she still refused to be checked. Then she went into labour, and a day later she was still labouring. She was at home with my stepmother and one of her sisters to support her. And then I dropped in.'

'To help?'

'I hadn't even been told she was due,' she said. 'When I arrived I realised Dad was in Auckland on business but they'd taken over the house as a birthing centre. I walked in and Sunrise was out of her mind with pain and exhaustion. There was bleeding and the baby was in dire trouble. I guess I just took over. I rang the ambulance and the hospital and warned them but I knew already... I'd listened... The baby's heartbeat was so faint...'

'The baby died?'

'They called her Sunset. How corny's that for a dying baby? She was suffering from a hypoxic brain injury and she died when she was three days old. Sunrise was lucky to survive. She won't be able to have more children.'

'So that makes you a baby killer?'

'I didn't know,' she said drearily, 'how much my stepmother really resented me until then. Or make that hate. I have no idea why, but at the coroner's inquest she stood in the witness stand and swore I'd told Sunrise it was safe. She swore I'd said everything was fine. I'd been the chosen midwife, she said, and my stepsisters concurred. Of course they would have gone to the hospital, they said, but one after another they told the court that I'd said they didn't need to.

'And you know what? My dad believed them. The coroner believed them. They came out of the court and Sunrise was crying, but my stepmother actually smirked. She tucked her arm in Dad's arm and they turned their backs on me. She's had her way after all this time. I'm finally right out of her family.'

Silence. More silence.

He shouldn't have asked, he thought. How to respond to a tragedy like this?

'My roller-derby team has asked me to quit,' she said into the dark. 'My dad—or Barbie—employs two of the girls' partners. Some of my medical colleagues stand by me—they know what I would and wouldn't do—but the town's too small for me to stay. I'm on unpaid leave now but I know I'll have to go.'

'So you've come to the great metropolis of Hideaway.' His fingers remained on her hair, just touching. Just stroking. 'I can see the logic.'

'I needed time out.'

'What are you writing?'

'Writing?

'By the fire. While I was snoozing.'

'That's none of your business,' she said, shocked.

'Sorry. Diary? No, I won't ask.' He hesitated for all of two seconds. 'Did you put something nice about me in it?'

'Only how much you weigh. Like a ton.' The mood had changed again. Lightness had returned. Thankfully.

'That's not kind,' he said, wounded.

'It's what matters. My shoulder's sore.'

'My leg's worse.'

'Do you need more painkillers? We can double the dose.'

'Yes, please,' he said, even though a hero would have knocked them back. Actually, a hero would have put her aside, braved a cyclone or two, swum to the mainland and knocked the heads of her appalling family together. A hero might do that in the future but for now his leg did indeed hurt. Knocking heads together needed to take a back seat. But it wouldn't be forgotten, he promised himself. Just shelved.

'If I have hurt your shoulder…you can take painkillers too.'

'I'm on duty.'

'You're not on duty,' he told her, gentling again. 'You need to sleep.'

'In a cyclone?'

'This isn't a cyclone. This is an edge of a cyclone.'

'Then I don't want to see a centre.'

'Hopefully we won't,' he said. 'Hopefully when we wake it'll have blown out to sea.'

'Hope on,' she said, and sat up and found him a couple of pills.

'Mary?'

'Mmm?'

'Sleep with me.'

'I don't seem to have a choice,' she said, and settled down again, and when he tugged her to him and held her, she didn't pull away.

At dawn the cyclone hit square on, and even in the safety of the cave the world seemed like it was exploding.

Afterwards she read that winds had reached two hundred miles an hour or more. They couldn't measure precisely because the instruments had been blown from their exposed eyrie on a neighbouring island. All Mary knew was that when she woke it sounded like a hundred freight trains were thundering right over, under and into their cave.

The wind was blasting from behind the cave but with such ferocity that the cave entrance was a vortex, sucking things in. Sand, grit, leaves. Their makeshift bed was far back, out of harm's way, or she'd thought out of harm's way, but who could tell with such a force?

The noise was unbelievable. The pressure in the cave was

unbelievable. Heinz was under the quilt, as far down as he could get, whimpering in terror.

Mary felt like joining him.

'It's all noise and bluster.' Ben's arm was around her, holding her tight against him, and his voice was a deep rumble over-riding terror. 'I don't think we're on the outside any more,' he said, his voice amazingly calm in her ear. 'Cyclone Lila's huffing and puffing and threatening to blow our house down, but she won't succeed. She won't because my heroine, the amazing Smash 'em Mary, found us a cave. We're surrounded by nice thick rock. We're safe, no matter what she hurls at us.'

She hurled a tree. Mary heard it crash against the cliffs. In the dim light at the cave entrance she saw the trunk slide sideways across the cave mouth, and Ben might have thought he was holding her but now she was holding him. Tight. Hard. She might be safe in her cave but this was something out of this world.

She clung. She clung and clung and clung.

The world was ending. Dawn might be breaking on a new day somewhere in the world but dawn was breaking here on catastrophe. She was expecting her cave to implode. She was expecting her island to pick up its roots and head for England.

So much for being nurse in charge. Ben had a head injury and a leg injury. She should be doing hourly obs, asking solicitous questions about his health.

All she could do was cling.

'You're safe,' he said into her ear, and when he was this close she believed him.

She clung. Skin against skin. His warmth and strength were the only things that mattered.

He was in boxers. She was in bra and panties. His body was rough against hers, and warm, and it was the only thing between her and catastrophe.

The noise was unbelievable. It felt like the entire world had been picked up and was blowing away. Even the ground under them seemed to be trembling, and their bodies were reacting accordingly.

She was no longer in charge of her body.

What were the needs on the Maslow scale? Food first and shelter, but sex was right up there.

If she buried herself in his body the noise would stop, but it seemed more than that. Much more.

If she'd been lying with a stranger, surely it wouldn't be like this, but Ben seemed no stranger. What was it between them? Danger, isolation, but more. She didn't know and she didn't have time to think it through. All she knew was that she was in this man's arms and she wanted him.

For this moment, this fragment of time, there was nothing but this man. There was no thought of the past or the future. For now, the only escape from the storm was Ben.

Less than twenty-four hours ago he'd thought he was going to die. He'd almost drowned. He was black with bruises. His leg was still giving him hell, but he was holding a woman in his arms and the pain and terror of the past couple of days was fading to nothing.

All that mattered was her.

Was this casual sex? Was this a fast mating because it was offered—for it *was* offered. He could feel her need.

The noise of the storm outside was unbelievable. She was holding him for comfort; she needed his strength, his warmth, his presence.

But this was more than that. She was holding him as if she'd merge with him.

This was more than casual sex.

Maybe he'd say that to himself, he thought, or he tried to think as his arms drew her closer, as her skin pressed against his skin. Her breasts were moulding to him, the slivers of her lace bra almost non-existent. She was the most beautiful creature he'd ever held.

The most beautiful woman…

Was that the storm talking? The adrenalin of the cyclone?

He pulled away and it nearly killed him. He put her at arm's length so he could look into those beautiful, wounded eyes.

This was a wounded creature hiding from the world.

This was a woman whose past resonated with his.

Nonsense. He was the indulged son of serious money. His family connections had always made life easy for him.

But her loneliness resonated with him in such a way…

But this wasn't loneliness. This was urgent physical need, and even if it killed him he would not take advantage of this woman.

'Mary, think,' he managed. 'I can't…stop. Mary, are you sure?'

'That I want your body?' Her voice was surprisingly calm. 'I'm as sure as I've ever been in my life.'

'I don't suppose…' His voice didn't match hers. It was ragged with want and there was no way he could disguise it. 'That you carry condoms in that nurse's bag?'

'You didn't pack some in your lifejacket pocket before you jumped overboard?' Her words might be light but the jagged need, the need that matched his, was unmistakeable.

'I can't think why not, but no.'

'So…so no diseases I should know about?'

'No, but—'

'Then I want you,' she said, as simply as that, and it took his breath away. 'Consequences can hang themselves.'

'Mary…'

'Mmm? She was holding him, her fingers touching his spine, her body pressing against him. Blocking out everything but the feel of her. 'How…how old is Heinz?'

She managed a chuckle. 'Old enough not to be shocked. And in case you hadn't noticed, it's pretty dark.'

'That's a relief,' he managed, and tugged her tighter still. 'Heinz, close your eyes. Your mistress and I are about to block one storm out with another.'

CHAPTER FIVE

THEY PRETTY MUCH clung to one another for twelve hours. That was how long it took for the cyclone to blast their slice of paradise to pieces.

It didn't matter, though, Ben thought in the moments he could surface to thinking. For now, for this time out of reality, he felt like he'd found his home.

Outside the cyclone shrieked across and around the island, doing its worst, while they made love and talked in whispers right against each other's ears because that was the only way they could be heard.

There was a couple of hours' eerie silence as the eye passed over. Mary suggested pulling apart then, checking the beach, thinking if something...someone else had been washed up... But Ben knew no one could have survived in a sea rougher than the pre-cyclonic conditions he'd been washed up in, and how did they know how long the eye would take to pass?

With his injured knee he couldn't move fast, and the thought of his Mary—*his Mary?*—being caught up in it was unbearable.

Then the darkness and the wind closed in on them once more and the quilt was their refuge again.

Their bodies were their refuge.

Heinz was there, too. Every now and then the little dog squirmed upwards as if to make sure his mistress was still there, head as well as toes. Then he'd retreat to the warmth of the nest their feet made—as if he knew they needed privacy.

Privacy? Ben had never felt so private.

He was a loner. His parents' appalling marriage, the family

wealth that set him and Jake apart, had turned him into himself. He'd moved into his father's financial world almost by default. There'd been no one else to take on his father's role as head of such a vast financial empire, but in the end he'd found it suited him.

He discovered he had a talent for finance, and the financial world was superficial enough to suit him. Emotion had no place. He moved in sophisticated circles, with women who were content to partner him for appearances. They knew not to intrude on his solitude.

And yet this slip of a girl had broken through. How? He didn't know, and for now he didn't care.

They talked and made love, talked again, then fell into a half-sleep where their bodies seemed to merge closer than he'd felt to anyone in his life. Closer than he'd imagined he could feel.

She asked questions and he answered, and vice versa. There seemed no boundaries. The storm had blasted them away.

He found himself talking of his childhood, of the isolation he and Jake had found themselves in, how one dare had led to another. He told her of an understanding nanny who'd said, 'Guys, you don't need to kill yourselves to get your parents to notice you.' And then she'd added, sadly, 'Your parents are so caught up in their own worlds, you mightn't manage it no matter what you do.'

Those words had been spoken when he was about twelve. They hadn't made one whit of difference to the risks he and Jake had taken, but thinking back…

His mother's demands that her children cheer her up, make her happy, pander to her emotions. Her eventual suicide when they'd failed. The appalling distant cruelty of his father. Their childhood behaviour made sense now, and here in this cocoon of passion and warmth and safety he could say it.

But he didn't need to say it. It was just one of the passing thoughts that went between them, and it was as if he was lying in the dark, totally isolated, talking to himself.

Or not.

Because she listened and she held him, and the words were absorbed and held. Somehow, within that cocoon, he felt the armour around his heart soften and crack.

Just for now. Just for this storm. They both knew there was no tomorrow. Was that part of the deal?

'Tell me about roller derby,' he said at one point, and he felt her body lighten. A frisson of laughter seemed to pass between them.

What was it with this woman? If she smiled, he seemed to smile with her. His body seemed to react to hers, no matter what she did.

They seemed…one.

It was the storm, he told himself. Shared danger. The emotion and peril of the last two days. It was nothing more.

But somehow, right now, it seemed much more.

'Roller derby's my home,' she said, and he blinked.

'Pardon?'

'You went into the army,' she said. 'I'm guessing roller derby's the same thing for me. Nice, little Mary, goody two shoes, knocked down whenever I do anything that might be noticed because I have a powerful stepmother and three overwhelming stepsisters. But when I put on my skates, I can be someone else. I can be the me I suspect I could have been if my mum had lived.'

'So when you put your skates on, you're Bad Ass Mary.'

'Smash 'em Mary,' she corrected him. 'I can do anything when I have my team around me. The power is unbelievable, but there are no roadside bombs for the unwary.'

'Only the odd broken leg.'

'I've never broken anything. I'm little and quick and smart.'

He could see that about her. It made him smile again.

'And rough?'

'You'd better believe it.'

'I'd love to watch you play.'

'That's not going to happen.' He heard her smile die.

'You'll find another team.'

'Another team, another town, another life?'

'Mary…' He rolled over and tugged her close.

'Mmm?'

'That's for tomorrow. Not now. Now is just…now.'

'I should stop thinking about it?'

'Yes.'

'I need distraction.'

'I'm good at distraction,' he said, and kissed her. He kissed her as she should be kissed, this wiry, tough, soft, vulnerable, yet ready-to-face-the-world warrior queen. 'I can provide distraction now. All you need to do is say yes.'

'Yes,' she whispered—and so he did.

She woke and there was silence.

Silence, silence and silence. It was so quiet it was almost loud.

She was cocooned against Ben's body, enfolded and protected, and for a couple of dreamy moments she found herself wishing she could stay. But the silence told her this time out was almost over.

Any minute now the world would break in. They'd be rescued, she could pick up the pieces and start again.

A consummation devoutly to be wished?

No. She didn't wish. All she wished was right here, right now. She closed her eyes and let herself savour Ben's body. Life was all about now, she told herself. She refused to think further.

'Mary?'

'Mmm?' Shut up, she was pleading beneath her breath. Don't you know that if we wake up it's over?

'It's over,' he said, and she kept her eyes closed for one last millisecond, gathering her resources, such as they were.

She could do this.

'We've survived,' she said, and she thought, I will survive. And then she thought, How dramatic is that? Woman who's just had a magnificent time out with a wounded warrior; celebrating survival? She felt like she should be celebrating much more.

She could put him in her book. Who was she kidding? He already *was* in her book.

And who was she kidding with her writing? Writing would give her an alternative career? That was fantasy.

Like now. But fantasy was over.

Ben was putting her gently away, kissing her with all the tenderness in the world but then setting her back, holding her shoulders so he could look into her eyes.

'That was a very nice way to spend the storm,' he said, and she managed a smile.

'Diversional therapy? They taught us that at nursing school. It works beautifully.'

'You never learned what we just did at nursing school.'

'I… No.'

'Mary, if there are consequences…'

'There won't be consequences.' She said it with more confidence than she felt. It was the wrong time of the month, she should be okay, but…but…

But there were things she could do. She just had to be practical.

'I'll always be here for you,' he said, and there was that in his voice that said he meant it. 'No matter where you are in the world, if you ever need me…'

'If ever I wash up on a beach…'

'I'm not joking,' he said, and touched her lips gently with his fingers. 'I'm yours for life.'

He meant he had a lifelong debt, she thought. Yours for life? No and no and no. Already she could see him moving on.

'We need a radio,' he said.

'There's been no transmission since before I found you. I suspect the mainland transmission towers have gone.'

'Phone?' he said without much hope.

'Same. But I turned mine off, conserving the battery so when it does come on again I can call.'

She saw his relief. 'You normally get reception?'

'From higher on the island, where the hut is.' She hauled

herself together, trying to ignore the feel of his hands on her shoulders, trying to ignore the part of her that was screaming that she didn't want to leave this place.

She had to leave.

'I'll do a recce,' she said. 'Heinz and me. It's time he got some exercise.'

'*We'll* do a recce.'

'Yeah, Commando Sir,' she said dryly. 'Have you seen the size of your knee?'

'It's better.'

'It's straight. It's not better. And there's no proof you don't have a broken bone. You want to be on the other side of the island and the bone shifts? What good would that do either of us?'

'I need to find out what's happened to Jake,' he said, and she knew his focus had gone out of this cave, back to the most important thing in the world.

His twin.

He'd moved on. She must, too.

She sat up and stared out into the bright morning light. The sky was clear, the wind had dropped to almost nothing, and she could see the turquoise blue of the bay. 'The tide looks like it's out,' she said. 'There'll be a couple of hours when I can access most parts of the beach. What if you stay here and tend the fire, and Heinz and I will do a circumnavigation of the island. We'll check and see what's left of the hut but we'll check the beach first.'

She very carefully didn't look at his face. She stared out to sea as if she wasn't thinking about anything at all except maybe finding the odd interesting shell. 'It'd be good to see what the storm's washed up,' she said in a voice that said she was hardly interested.

He wasn't fooled for a moment. 'Mary...'

She dropped the pretence. 'I know you're worried. You shouldn't be. He was in a harness. Those choppers don't drop anyone.'

'Thank you,' he said. He was trying to believe her but he

was also thinking of next worst-case scenarios. 'Mary, there were others…'

'I'll be looking. I'm not Jake-specific. Any more commando heroes washed overboard, I'll tug 'em home.'

'Isn't one enough?'

'One's more than enough,' she said, and then, because she couldn't help herself, she took his face between her hands and she kissed him. She kissed him strongly and surely, and he wasn't to know that for her it seemed like a goodbye.

'One's more than enough,' she said. 'One's given me strength that should keep me going for a long, long time.'

'How long?'

'I'd guess a few hours,' she said, forcing herself to put the kiss aside as it was too hard to think about. 'It normally takes two hours to walk the beach but with the debris it might take me four. Don't expect me home for lunch.'

'For better or worse but not for lunch?'

'That's right, dear,' she said, and grinned. 'I'll take an apple and a water bottle. Meanwhile, you keep the home fires burning and have my slippers warmed and ready. Bye.'

She left, taking Heinz with her, and he wanted to go with her so much it almost killed him. Only practicalities stopped him. His leg would impede them both. He did need her to go right round the island. He did need her to check the shore.

Just in case.

But she was right. Harnesses didn't fail. Jake would be safe. He was being paranoid.

And now, on top of his worry for Jake, another worry was superimposed. Mary, pushing her way through debris, navigating a cyclone-devastated island…

What if she fell?

She wouldn't. What had she said? She was little and quick and smart.

She was, too.

His warrior woman.

He smiled. Mary. He owed her so much. How could he ever repay her?

Do something about her appalling family?

What?

He threw a couple more logs on the fire and thought about the sequence of events leading to the coroner's verdict. Had she employed a lawyer? He bet she hadn't. A lawyer would have cross-examined, produced times and witnesses outside the family, talked about pre-existing family conflict.

Would Mary allow him to push for a rehearing? Would she allow him to do that for her?

He suspected not. He could hear the defeat in her voice, but also the loyalty. Somewhere there was a father she still loved, and these appalling women were his wife and daughters.

What else? He'd never felt so helpless.

She'd been gone for half an hour, far too early for her to return, yet already he was imagining worst-case scenarios. There'd been trees ripped, maybe landslides from so much rain. So many hazards...

Things on the beach.

Jake...

In desperation he picked up the papers she'd been writing on. He'd watched her, half asleep, and seen the intent look on her face. It had seemed like this was something that took her out of her current misery.

'None of your business.' She'd said it loud and clear.

It was none of his business. He owed her privacy but he was going out of his mind.

He hauled himself outside to sit in the sun, acknowledging as he did just how swollen his leg was; how impossible it was that he do anything useful.

He stared out over the storm-swept island, at the flattened trees, at the mountain of debris washed up on the beach.

Jake.

Mary.

It was too much. He hauled himself back inside to fetch the papers.

It was none of his business. He acknowledged it, but he started to read anyway.

Negotiating the beach was a nightmare. The cyclone had caused storm surges and the water had washed well up the cliff face. She looked at the new high-water mark and shuddered. If she hadn't found Ben when she had...

Don't go there, she told herself. It made her feel ill.

Surely no one else could have survived, but she had to check. The debris washed up was unbelievable—and some of it looked as if it had come from the yacht fleet.

Every time she saw a flash of something that shouldn't be there, a hint of colour, waterproof clothing, shattered fibreglass or ripped sails, her heart caught in her mouth. No bodies, she pleaded as she searched. No Jake? He had to have been rescued.

What sort of people manned those rescue helicopters? she wondered, thinking suddenly about the woman who'd been dangling in a harness with the unknown Jake. There was a prayer in her heart for both of them—indeed, for anyone who'd been out there.

But even before she'd found Ben, the radio had said people had died.

She searched on and stupidly, weirdly, she found herself crying. Why? Tears wouldn't help anyone. She was Mary, the practical one. Mary, who didn't do emotion.

Mary, who'd just spent twenty-four hours in a stranger's arms?

She didn't feel like Mary any more. Over the past months she'd been blasted out of her nice, safe existence, first by the death of her stepsister's baby, then by a storm—and now by a man holding her as if he cared.

He was shocked and frantic about his brother's safety. He'd been using her body to forget.

'And I was using him,' she told Heinz. She was sitting on a massive tree trunk washed up on the beach, retrieving her apple from her backpack.

But he'd held her as if he cared. No one did that. Even her father…

Don't go there. She'd loved her father as much as she'd loved her mother. Her mother's death had been unavoidable.

Her father's marriage to Barbie had meant desertion and she'd never truly trusted anyone since.

She stared down at her apple, but she didn't feel like eating. What was she doing, dredging up long-ago pain?

She wanted, quite desperately, to be back on the mainland, surrounded by her roller-derby team. She needed a fast, furious game where she could pit her wits and her strength against skills that matched hers—where she had no room to think of anything beyond the physical.

As she'd been when she'd lain in Ben's arms?

Only there'd been room for more than the physical with Ben. It had felt like there was far more.

And there wasn't. She didn't need anyone. Hadn't her whole life taught her that?

'So get over it. Get over him.' She crunched her apple with unnecessary force. Heinz looked at her with worry, and she bit off a piece and offered it.

He wasn't interested. He headed back into the kelp. Here be dead fish and stuff. Here be something better than apples.

'That's what I get for hauling your dog food to the cave,' she retorted. 'Some dogs would be grateful for apple.'

Her words caught her sense of the ridiculous and she managed a half-hearted smile. It was only half-hearted, though. She truly was discombobulated. In the last couple of months her world had been blasted apart, and the cyclone seemed the culmination.

Wrong. Ben seemed the culmination.

He was a fast reader but sometimes he slowed. Sometimes he wanted to soak in each word.

He'd desperately needed an escape from his worry about

Jake. Last night Mary had been that escape. Now the manu-script in his hands was giving him a lesser one.

His dark, shadowed eyes, grey and mysterious, seemed to bore into parts of her she hadn't even known existed. They seemed to see the wolf within.

He got it. He was grinning with delight as he recognised himself. She'd gone back and crossed a few things out in the backstory. His build, his eyes, his physique, were superimposed on...her hero?

This man was supposed to be a twin? Heaven help her if there were two of them. One was enough to make a were-wolf run for cover.

He read on, entranced. Escape... That's what this woman was all about, he thought, and she was very, very good at it. Her writing was part of her. The whole was entrancing.

She rounded the entire island. She found storm-blasted birds, some dead but most simply stunned and battered, hunkering down while they recovered.

She—or rather Heinz—found dead fish. Heinz let the birds be but not the fish. How much fish could one dog eat? Mary was past caring.

Thank God, no bodies.

Finally she made her way inland to check on the hut. But what hut? The base of the fireplace was all that was left. The tin roof was scattered through the bushland. The timber walls had crumbled. Her friends' possessions were sodden and ru-ined. There seemed nothing left for her to save.

'And we've probably ruined the quilt as well,' she told Heinz.
'I'll fix it.'

Ben's voice in the stillness made her jump. She turned and

he was sitting on a fallen tree at the edge of the clearing, watching her.

'You shouldn't have come,' she said, shocked. 'You should be resting your knee.'

'You've been gone for four hours,' he said pointedly. 'A man's allowed to get worried. Two stout walking-sticks and I managed.'

'How did you know where to come?'

'There are two paths from the cave. One leads to the beach. I figured the other led here, and I figured this was where you'd end up. I'm up there with Einstein,' he said proudly.

She managed a smile. He looked astonishing. His face was battered, the shirt and pants he was wearing had the odd rip, he'd wrapped his one bare foot in a ripped towel to form a makeshift shoe, but he looked...healthy?

Maybe more than healthy, she conceded. He looked more tough, rugged and good-looking than any man had a right to look.

Especially when a woman had to be sensible.

Think about something else, she told herself desperately. *Focus.* She gazed around the clearing at the mess.

Nothing occurred. She just wanted to look at him.

'I'll have the quilt cleaned,' he told her. 'Restored if necessary. I'll have this cottage rebuilt if insurance doesn't pay for it. I'll do anything in my power to pay for what you've done for me. Starting with the quilt.'

'How did you know the quilt's important?'

'I've seen homes destroyed in Afghanistan. I've seen women who've lost all their possessions, and I've seen what a tiny thing can mean.' He smiled at her, but his smile had changed. All the compassion in the world was in that smile. 'After you left I had a chance to take a good look at that quilt. It's amazing.'

'Barbara's grandmother sewed it for her trousseau.'

Some time during the last twenty-four hours she'd told him about Barbara and Henry.

Some time in the last twenty-four hours she'd told him almost everything.

'There's not a lot here we can salvage,' he said, and she didn't reply. There wasn't any need.

'The boat?' he asked, without much hope.

'Smashed.'

'You didn't think to put it somewhere safe?'

She flashed him a look.

He grinned. 'Yeah, I know. Lack of forethought is everywhere. I should have put my yacht in dry dock in Manhattan.'

'The world's full of should-haves.'

'But on the other hand, I brought crackers, cheese and chocolate with me from the cave,' he said, and she looked up at his lopsided hopeful expression and she couldn't help smiling. He was playing the helpful Labrador.

And suddenly she thought… Cellar.

Henry had told her about the cellar, almost as an aside, when he'd been describing the house. 'There's a dugout under the washhouse,' he said. 'Accessed by a trapdoor. I keep a few bottles there if you're desperate.'

Did this qualify as desperate?

She left Ben and headed for where the washhouse had been. She hauled a few timbers aside and after a couple of moments Ben hobbled across to help.

'We're looking for?'

'Desperate measures,' she said.

'Sorry?'

'Desperate times call for desperate measures. I'll make it up to Henry somehow.' She hauled the last piece of timber aside and exposed a trapdoor with a brass ring.

Ben tugged it up. It was a hole, four feet wide, maybe three feet deep.

'You could have hidden in here during the storm,' he said.

'Yeah, right. Four feet by four feet, filled with a hundred or so bottles of wine.'

'After the first twenty you wouldn't have noticed you were

squashed.' He lifted out the first bottle and stared. 'Wow. Your friends have good taste.'

'It'll take me a month's salary to pay them back but this might be worth it.'

'I told you, I'm paying.' He lifted the next bottle out and eyed it with reverence. 'I've been trying to think of the perfect wine to go with crackers, cheese and chocolate. I think I've found it.'

'You think we dare?'

'I know we dare,' Ben said. 'My leg hurts. This is for medicinal purposes, if nothing else. And, Mary, I suspect you're hurting, too,' he said, and suddenly his voice gentled again. 'Carting me up that beach was no mean feat. You must be aching, and inside there's probably almost as much hurt as I'm carrying. I think we need this wine, Nurse Hammond. I think we both need all the help we can get.'

They sat on a sun-drenched log, looked out over the battered island, ate their crackers and cheese, and drank amazing wine.

The cheese was a bit dry and the glassware left a bit to be desired. Every glass in the cottage had been broken but a couple of ancient coffee mugs had survived the carnage.

It didn't matter. The food tasted wonderful. The wine—stunning even in different circumstances—couldn't have tasted better if it was drunk from exquisite crystal.

They didn't talk. There seemed no need.

They were perched on a ledge overlooking the entire west of the island. Every tree seemed to have been shattered or flattened. The beach was a massive mound of litter. The sea still looked fierce, an aftermath of the storm, but the sun was on their faces. The world around them had been destroyed but for now, for this moment, all was peace.

Heinz had been lying at Mary's feet. He suddenly stood, staggered a few feet away—and brought up half a fish.

'Nice,' Ben said.

'I reckon he ate about six,' Mary told him, grimacing. 'There may be more to come.'

'He might have chewed them before he swallowed.'

'He was a stray when I found him. He eats first and asks questions later. Even essential questions, like "Can I fit it in?" or "Is it edible?"'

'Really nice,' Ben said, and then, when Heinz looked wistfully down at his half-fish, he stirred, grabbed a stick, gouged a hole in the sodden earth and buried it.

Then, at the look on Heinz's face, he shoved the stick deep in the ground and tied a piece of ripped curtain at the top.

'*X* marks the spot,' he told Heinz. 'Come the revolution, you know where it's buried.'

'Nice,' Mary intoned back at him, and their eyes met and suddenly they were laughing.

It felt…amazing.

It felt free.

And Mary thought, for all the drama and tension of the last couple of days, she was feeling better than she'd felt for months.

Or years?

Because she'd made abandoned love to a guy she hardly knew?

But she did know him, she thought. She watched the laughter in his eyes, she watched the way he fondled Heinz's floppy ears, she saw the tension in his face that could never be resolved until he knew his brother was safe, and she thought…she did know this man.

Somehow in the last twenty-four hours he seemed to have become part of her.

And that was crazy, she told herself. Any minute now the world would break in, and part of her would disappear back to Manhattan.

Besides, she didn't do relationships. She'd trusted her father with her whole heart and he'd turned his back on her. His back was still turned. How did you walk away from something like that?

'I read your book,' he said, and she froze.

'You read…'

'Werewolves and dragons—and me.' He grinned. 'Entirely satisfactory.'

She was on her feet but feeling like the earth was opening under her. Her writing... It had always been her escape. This man had read it? 'You had no right...'

'I know,' he confessed. 'But I was bored. Do you mind?'

'I don't show my writing to anyone.' It was part of her, the part she disappeared into when life got too hard. That he'd seen it...

'You should. It's great.'

'It's fantasy.'

'I suspected that,' he said gravely. 'I haven't exactly learned how to handle a six-pronged sword in real life.'

She closed her eyes.

'Mary, I really am sorry,' he said. 'You look like... It seems important. I shouldn't have intruded. I shouldn't have looked.'

He shouldn't have looked into her? What was it about this man? He was seeing...all of her.

She opened her eyes again met his gaze. Straight and true. Where had that phrase come from?

He was a man to be trusted?

Maybe she had no choice. She'd already exposed so much.

Deep breath. What would a normal...writer...say if someone had read their work? 'You think it's over the top?' she tried, cautiously, and he seemed to relax.

'It is over the top and it's great.' He grinned. 'A few more thousand words and the publication world awaits.'

'Don't mock.'

'I'm not mocking,' he said, and there was that look again. Straight and true. 'Mary, it's awesome.' Then his face changed, to an expression she could hardly understand. 'I think you're awesome,' he added. 'I wish there were some dragons I could slay on your behalf in real life.'

This was doing her head in. Any minute now she'd step forward and take this man and hold him.

She didn't do relationships. She didn't trust.

She could trust this man?

'M-meanwhile, we need to figure how to get off this island,' she managed, and heaven only knew the effort it took to get the words out.

'We do,' he said ruefully. 'Fantasy's great, but the real world awaits us.'

'It does,' she agreed, and then she muttered an aside. 'I just need to keep remembering it.'

CHAPTER SIX

THE REAL WORLD broke in half an hour later.

Helicopters appeared in the distance, buzzing out over the islands but mostly out to sea.

'The yacht race was a disaster,' Ben said as they watched them. 'That's who they'll be looking for. The race was full of idiots like us, in expensive boats but not enough skills to cope.'

'How many sailors have the skills to cope with a cyclone?'

'We could have done better. I never questioned the seaworthiness of the life raft. The salesman told me it was state of the art. I knew how to set it up but it never occurred to me that it was little more than a giant beach ball. I just hope other yachts had better equipment.' He shaded his eyes, watching a couple of dots of helicopters flying out on the horizon. 'If they're still searching, I hope whoever they're looking for had a better life raft than ours.'

'They're probably looking for you.'

'Or Jake.'

'Let's face probabilities, shall we?' she said astringently. 'At last report, Jake was being winched to safety. You, on the other hand, were drifting in a beach ball. So they're looking for you. Driftwood. Matches, fire, smoke. Stat. We need to get smoke up there fast before the weather closes in again.'

'Is the weather closing in?'

'Who knows? I hope someone, somewhere is working frantically to restore a transmission tower but nothing's coming through on my radio. Or my phone.' She flicked her cellphone out of her pocket. 'Dead.'

'Is it charged?'

'You tell me to try turning it off and on again and I'll tell you where to put it, tech-head.' She tossed him the phone. 'Here. You play with the on and off buttons, then make your way back to the cave at your leisure. I'm off to try a less tech-heavy form of communication.'

'Mary...'

She'd started to turn away but she stopped and looked back at him. 'Yes?'

'Thank you,' he said simply, and they were a mere two words but all the power in the universe was behind them. He looked at her, just looked. Their gazes held for a long, long moment, and in the end it seemed to tear something when she had to turn away.

'My pleasure,' she managed, but as she headed back to the cave she felt those stupid tears slipping down her face again.

What was wrong with her? Smash 'em Mary was turning into a wuss.

There was a part of Smash 'em Mary that didn't even want the helicopter to come.

Only the helicopter did come. The fire took hold and she covered it with green leaves. Smoke billowed upwards, the chopper changed course and headed toward them.

Ben had made his way back by then, limping heavily, using his sticks for support. She should have moved slowly, staying to help him, but rescue had seemed more important.

Of course it was.

They stood in silence as the chopper approached. There seemed little to say, or maybe there was lots to say but neither of them could think what.

There was no way the chopper could land. The island was hilly, and the beach, normally a possible landing place, was a mess. The chopper came in low, assessing the situation, and then someone came down a rope.

A guy, Ben noted. Neither was it the chopper that had taken

Jake away. Why not? His stomach clenched, thinking of the chopper in that wild weather. Surely if it had survived…

'That's called catastrophising,' Mary said. 'Stop it.'

'How did you know…?'

'Your face is like an open book. Just because this isn't the chopper that took Jake, it doesn't mean Jake's at the bottom of the sea. I know you think New Zealand's tiny compared to the US, but we do run to more than one helicopter.'

He managed a smile and then the guy on the rope landed near them, and she headed forward to help.

Ben stayed where he was. He'd pushed too hard. His leg seemed like it was at the end of its useful life. He'd never felt so useless.

Jake…

'Take Ben first,' Mary was saying.

He roused himself and thought, *What?*

'She tells me you're injured, sir,' the paramedic said. 'Do we need to splint your leg before we move you? Any other injuries?'

'I don't think he wants to be stretchered up,' Mary said, and she was smiling.

He wasn't smiling.

'My brother…' he said, and the paramedic's face grew grim.

'You're one of the race crew?'

'Yes.'

'We're very pleased to see you,' he said. 'There are still crew members missing.' He turned to Mary, obviously forming a question, but she answered before he could ask.

'I've searched the beach and found no one.'

'Could someone have made their way inland?'

'If they were capable of getting inland they'd have found the remains of the hut. It's the obvious high point.'

'It's probably worth sending a team over to look more thoroughly,' the guy said, 'if this one's washed up.

This one. This victim.

Ben was going out of his mind.

'Do you know if my brother's safe?' he demanded. 'Jake Logan. He was pulled up on a chopper before the cyclone hit.'

'That'll have been a New Zealand crew,' the guy told him. 'We're Australian. I don't know who they did and didn't pull off.'

'The choppers are all safe?'

'I don't know that either,' he said apologetically. 'This is our first run. Please, our time's short.'

He didn't need to say more. Others were missing. He had to get back in the air.

'Put the harness on,' Mary said, and something inside him snapped.

'No,' he said. 'You go first and that's an order. I'll grab your manuscript and follow.'

'It's not important.'

'It is. Go!'

'Blimey,' the guy said, obviously astounded at the vehemence behind his words. 'Women and children first? The island's not sinking, mate.'

It wasn't, but the memory of Jake was all around him. He didn't know where Jake was. He wanted Mary safe.'

'You go first and I'll bring Heinz and the manuscript up with me,' he told Mary, and Mary looked at him as if he was out of his mind.

'You're the one with the bang on his head and the gammy leg. You're planning on holding my dog and my book while you air-swing? In your dreams, mister.'

The chopper guy sighed. 'Quiet dog?'

'He's eaten so many dead fish this morning he won't raise a wriggle,' Mary told him. 'But I wouldn't squeeze him.'

The guy grinned. 'Name?'

'Heinz.'

'I might have known. Okay, boys and girls, I'm taking the dog up while you sort the remaining order between you. No domestics while I'm away. Sheesh, the stuff we heroes have to put up with. Heinz, come with me while Mummy and Daddy sort out their rescue priorities.'

* * *

She went first, clutching the battered quilt. 'Because Barbara will forgive me everything but losing this.'

He came after, with her manuscript. He'd spent time in choppers in Afghanistan. He didn't like the memories.

He was hauled into the chopper and Mary was belted onto the bench. She was holding Heinz as if she needed him for comfort. She looked somehow... diminished?

Lost.

She'd come to the island to escape, he remembered. Now she was going home.

He sat beside her but she wouldn't look at him. She buried her face in Heinz's rough coat and he thought suddenly of the streams of refugees he'd seen leaving war zones.

Surely that was a dumb comparison—but the feeling was the same.

He touched her shoulder but she pulled away.

'Um, no,' she said, and she straightened and met his gaze full on. 'Thanks, Ben,' she said softly. 'But I'm on my own now.'

'You're not on your own.'

'This was a fairly dramatic time out,' she said. 'But it was just that. Time out. Now we both have stuff we need to face.' She shook herself then, and Smash 'em Mary took over. He saw the set of her chin, the flash of determination, the armour rebuilding. 'What I'm facing is nothing compared to you, but Jake will be okay. I'm sure of it.'

He had no room to respond.

In any other situation he would have...

Would have what? He didn't know.

For suddenly he was there again, in Afghanistan, watching a bloodied Jake being loaded onto the stretcher, knowing he couldn't go with the ambulance, knowing Jake's fate was out of his hands.

Loving brought gut-wrenching pain.

When he was fourteen years old his mother had suicided.

That day was etched into his mind so deeply he could never get rid of it.

Pain.

And here was this woman, sitting beside him, hurting herself. He'd forgotten his pain in her body. He'd used her.

He could love her.

Yeah, and expose him—and her—to more of the same? If he did...if he hurt her...

He hadn't been able to stop his mother's suicide. The emotional responsibility was too great.

Where was this going? He didn't have a clue. He only knew that he withdrew his hand from her shoulder, and when she inched slightly away he didn't stop her.

It was better to withdraw now. Kinder for both of them. He had relationships back in the US, of course he did, but the women he dated were strong, independent, never needy. They used him as an accessory and that was the way he liked it.

He never wanted a woman to need him.

'We're heading to Paihia,' the voice of the chopper pilot told them through their headphones. 'From there we'll have people help you, check you medically, find you somewhere to go.'

Mary nodded, a brisk little nod that told him more than anything else that she had herself contained again. She wasn't as strong as she made out, though, he thought. Strong, independent woman? Not so much.

It didn't matter, they were moving on.

It was what they both needed to do.

Paihia. A massive army clearing tent. People with clipboards, emergency personnel everywhere, reminding them both that they were bit-part players in a very big drama.

'Ben's hurt,' Mary managed, as a woman wearing medic insignia on her uniform met them off the chopper. 'I'm a nurse. He had a dislocated knee that I managed to put back in but it needs checking for possible fractures. He also had a bang on the head. I've pulled the cut together with steri-strips but it probably needs stitches.'

'We'll take it from here,' the medic said. 'And you?'

'I'm fine.'

'Can you come this way, sir? Would you like a wheelchair?'

'I don't need help,' he growled. 'I need to find my brother.'

'Your brother is?'

'Jake Logan. One of the yachties.'

'You're part of the round-the-world challenge?' Her face cleared. 'Thank God for that. They've lost so many, the organisers are frantic.'

That was a statement to make him feel better. Not.

'Jake…' he managed.

'The organisers have evacuated all survivors to Auckland,' she said. 'I don't have names.' She hesitated. 'We're sending a chopper with a couple of patients needing surgery in about ten minutes. If you let me do a fast check on your leg and head first, I can get you on that chopper.'

He turned and Mary was watching, still with that grave, contained face. The face that said she was moving on.

'Go, Ben,' she said. 'And good luck.'

'Where can I find you?'

'Sir…' the woman said.

The chopper was waiting.

'I need an address,' he told Mary. 'Now!'

'Email me if you like. I'm *MaryHammond400 at xmail dot com.*'

'*MaryHammond400?*'

'There's so many of us I got desperate.'

'There's only one of you.'

She smiled. 'It's nice of you to say so but there are millions of Marys in the world. Good luck with everything, Ben. Email me to let me know Jake's safe.'

'I will. And, Mary—'

'Just go.'

'Give me the quilt,' he told her, and she blinked, and he

thought bringing the quilt into the equation, a touch of practicality, threw her.

'You want it for a keepsake? You can't have it.'

'I'll have it restored for Barbara and send it back to you,' he told her. 'And I don't need keepsakes. Thank you, Mary 400. Smash 'em Mary. Mary in a million. I don't need keepsakes because I'll remember these last few days forever.'

She watched the chopper until it was out of sight. She hugged Heinz. She felt…weird.

She should feel gutted, she told herself. She felt like the man of her dreams was flying out of her life forever.

Only he wasn't. She even managed a wry smile. He'd been a dream, she decided, a break from the nightmare of the past. She was glad she'd made love with him. Abandoning herself in his body, she'd felt as if she'd shed a skin.

Was she now Mary 401?

'What can we do for you, Miss Hammond?' Another official with a clipboard was approaching, bustling and businesslike. 'Your American friends who own the island are frantic. We've fielded half a dozen calls. Would you like to ring and reassure them?'

'I'll do that,' she said, still feeling weird. 'I'll tell them their quilt's safe.'

'Is there someone else we can contact? You live in Taikohe. Can someone collect you?'

'Are the normal buses running?'

'Yes, but—'

'Then I'll take a bus.'

'I'm sure we can arrange someone to drive you. We have volunteers eager to help.'

'Thank you but no.' She took a deep breath. 'I need to put this behind me. Somehow life needs to get back to normal.'

CHAPTER SEVEN

New York

'MR LOGAN, THERE'S a Mary Hammond on the line, asking to see you. I told her you were fully booked but she says her business is personal. She's only in the country until Monday.'

Ben was knee deep in futures. The negotiations were complex and vital.

His secretary's words made the figures in front of him blur.

Mary Hammond.

Mary.

'Put her through.'

'She doesn't wish to speak to you on the phone,' Elspeth told him. 'She specifically said so. She's asking for a personal interview. Will I tell her no?'

His pen jabbed straight through a certificate with three wax seals on it. Three rather important seals, one of which was from a head of state. It didn't matter. 'I can see her now.'

There was a moment's silence while Elspeth returned to the outside line. His pen snapped.

'She can be here in an hour,' his secretary said, coming onto the line again. 'She's across town.'

'I'll send a car.'

'She's disconnected. Shall I delay the Howith negotiations?'

'Yes.'

'Will you need fifteen minutes? Half an hour?'

'I'll need the rest of the day,' Ben snapped. 'Cancel everything.'

His secretary disappeared, off to tell some of the world's top financiers that currency crises would have to wait. By the end of the day rumours would be flying. Ben Logan didn't miss appointments, not at this level.

But, then, Ben Logan had never been visited by the woman who'd saved his life.

He sat and stared at his desk and all he saw was Mary.

He should have flown back to the Bay of Islands to say goodbye, he conceded. He'd done all he could do, but still...

The days after the cyclone had been a blur. Getting off that chopper in Auckland. Walking over to that damned list.

Seeing Jake's name on the safe side.

Then he'd found Jake himself, in the admin office of the chopper company. He'd been shouting, offering to pay whatever it took, his entire fortune if necessary, to hire a chopper and head out to sea to personally look for Ben.

The look on his face when Ben walked in had been indescribable.

And then, of course, other things had superimposed themselves. Jake had insisted on doctors, on getting his knee checked.

Then a pub, late at night, and Jake saying quietly, 'Tell me about our mother.'

He'd remembered then the words he'd hurled at Jake as he'd forced his twin into being the one to leave the life raft. He'd finally thrown his mother's suicide into the equation.

'This is reality, Jake, not some stage play where you can play the hero. Face it now and move on. You're just like Mom. She couldn't face reality. Why do you think she killed herself?'

Until then it had been Ben's secret. Jake had been told she'd accidentally overdosed. Only Ben had known the truth, and twenty years on he hadn't enjoyed sharing.

They'd talked into the night, and drank, and things hadn't gotten easier. The pain of their mother's death was still bitter. Love... Ben didn't do it. He wouldn't. He never wanted that kind of pain again.

There was a reason the Logan boys walked alone. Jake had

tried and failed at marriage. The Logan men weren't meant for the soft side.

So even though he'd meant to go back and see Mary, in the end he'd decided it'd be better, kinder even, to make a clean break. The storm had only been that: a storm. It was over.

Except that the aftermath of that storm would be in his office in less than an hour.

Mary.

He hadn't quite managed to put her out of his head. On his laptop was a YouTube file, the final of the two top New Zealand roller-derby teams.

Smash 'em Mary was front and foremost, rolling for Taikohe. She was as she'd said, little, quick and smart, dodging girls twice her size, moving with lightning speed, taking her team to a win.

She'd played wearing fierce, warrior-woman make-up, black tights and purple socks, a tiny halterneck top and a short, short skirt.

The documents in front of him were important. He needed to concentrate.

He ended up watching the roller derby match, one more time.

If she didn't do this now, she never would.

It was crazy to come to the other side of the world just to talk to him. A telephone call would have worked, but it had taken courage to pick up the phone. Too much courage. She had to watch his face, she told herself, and in the end she'd decided it was the only way.

After all, it wasn't as if she hadn't had money for the fare, and that by itself needed personal thanks. Because three weeks after the storm a lawyer had appeared at the door of her cottage.

'Miss Hammond?'

'Yes?'

'Mr Ben Logan has sent me,' he told her. 'I'm Frank Blainey, QC, a lawyer specialising in defamation cases. Mr Logan has briefed me on a coroner's case that's put your career in jeopardy. He asked me to investigate. Miss Hammond, I've done some preliminary groundwork and frankly I'm appalled. Acting under Mr Logan's instructions, I've taken witness statements from individual members of your family, including your father, and from neighbours and colleagues.

'Because I've moved fast and interviewed in isolation, there's a clear case that we can take back to court. You have grounds for suing for perjury and defamation.'

She'd stood on the doorstep and forgotten to breathe. 'What… what…?'

'Take your time. It's big to take in, but I believe we've solved your problem.'

'Ben…Ben Logan?'

'He instructed me.'

'But I can't afford a QC.' It was a confused wail and the lawyer smiled.

'You have the Logan billions behind you. Whatever it takes, were Mr Logan's instructions, but in the end it's taken very little. You could have employed a lawyer yourself and got the same result.'

'But they're my family,' she whispered. 'My dad… I couldn't get up in court and call them liars.'

'Even when they are? Even though it has the potential to ruin your career?'

'I can't…'

'Well, I can,' he said, gently but firmly. 'And I have. Mr Logan seems to think you might not want to go to court again. If you don't wish it, I've arranged it another way. The witness statements are contradictory. I now have two colleagues' legal opinions that you have no case to answer.

'With your permission we'll present that to the nurses' registration body, together, if you wish, with your sworn statement that you don't wish your family to be put on trial for perjury. That will protect your job.

'As well as that, you've suffered significant financial and personal loss because of their perjury. Your stepmother has agreed to write this cheque on the grounds that you take it no further.'

He handed her the cheque. She looked at it and gasped.

'My father...' she managed.

The lawyer's tone gentled. 'I believe your father is appalled at the lies that have been told about you.' He hesitated. 'I don't believe he has the strength to stand up against your stepmother. He would wish to apologise but I doubt he will. He sees this cheque as an apology and he hopes you'll take it.'

It let them off the hook, she thought. She thought of all the lies, all the hurt.

Her father saw this cheque as an apology?

Standing there before the lawyer that Ben had sent, she thought suddenly that she'd never felt so alone.

Ben hadn't come to see her. He'd sent a lawyer.

Her father hadn't come to see her. He'd sent a cheque.

She was used to being alone, though. She could do this. She'd stood in the sun and forced herself to think of the ramifications of this money. Of the steps this lawyer—under Ben's instructions—had taken to help her.

'Ben asked you to do this?'

'He was aware you might think he has no right to interfere. I've done nothing except examine evidence in the public domain and present it to your family.'

'But on Ben's instructions.'

'On Mr Logan's instructions.'

It felt weird. It felt wrong. She was being paid off.

By Ben as well as her family?

It was a dumb thing to think. Unfair. But she stared at the cheque and thought of the difference it could make.

And she thought about a faint blue line—and she knew she needed to talk to Ben regardless.

'I'll tell Mr Logan you'll accept?' the lawyer asked.

'Thank you,' she said faintly. 'But I need to thank Mr Logan myself.'

So a month later, here she was, in Manhattan, in Logan House, a building whose foyer looked as it it'd swallow half of Taikohe. To say it was intimidating was to put it mildly.

'Mr Logan's waiting.' An efficient-looking woman in a crisp grey suit was waiting to escort her upstairs. 'There's to be no interruptions under any circumstances,' the woman told the receptionist. 'Mr Logan's orders. He's out for the rest of the day.'

'If he's busy…' Mary faltered.

'He's not busy for you, dear,' the woman said, and led the way.

Dear…

Did she look like someone who needed TLC?

'I bet she doesn't address company moguls as *dear*,' she muttered under her breath.

She should have dressed up more. She should have…turned corporate?

She was wearing her weddings and funerals suit. It was a bit old. She should have worn more make-up. She should have bought new shoes.

It didn't matter. She didn't belong here, no matter what she wore, and she wasn't here for corporate reasons.

The lift stopped at the highest floor. The door slid open, and the woman put a gentle hand in the small of her back to guide her out.

Bet she didn't do that to company moguls either.

But maybe she needed it. 'I don't…' To say panic was setting in was an understatement. 'I shouldn't…'

'Mr Logan's waiting,' the woman told her. She swung open the inner doors—and Ben was rising from a massive desk, walking forward to greet her.

Ben?

The last time she'd seen this man he'd been battered and wounded. He'd been in pain and he hadn't been sure if his twin was dead or alive. She'd held him in the storm and they'd taken and given comfort to each other.

But now…

This guy was a suit plus. No one she'd ever met wore a suit like this. It was deepest black with a fine grey pinstripe, and it fitted him as if it was moulded onto his beautiful body. It screamed quality, as did his gorgeous blue tie and the crisp white linen beneath it. Even his shoes screamed quality.

He was clean-shaven. His dark hair was neatly cut and immaculately groomed.

His shadowed grey eyes surveyed her from the toes up and she was reminded suddenly of an eagle, his fierce, intelligent eyes capable of seeing things no man should see.

She was imagining things. He was scaring her.

She shouldn't have come.

And then he smiled, striding towards her with his hands held out, and with his smile suddenly he was the Ben she'd held. The Ben she'd made love to.

'Mary,' he said, with all the welcome in the world. 'Smash 'em Mary, here in my office. I'm honoured.'

He hugged her fiercely but briefly and then held her at arm's length to look at her. Once more she got that sensation that he could see far more than she wished to tell him.

Ben.

She wanted a longer hug but after that one brief hold he was back under control.

How could she think she knew this man?

'Thanks, Elspeth,' Ben said.

And she thought, *This guy really is a billionaire.* Those two words had been a dismissal to his secretary, mild and brief, but the authority behind them had been absolute.

He was a man in command of his world—and what a world!

In the last weeks she'd looked him up on the internet—of course she had. His brother Jake the actor was famous. Ben seemed to fly under the radar but his business credentials were so impressive they'd made her gasp.

She thought of the cheque her father and stepmother had given her and what a difference it was making in her life.

This guy's fortune was enough to make her eyes water.

How could she possibly tell him what she needed to tell him without him taking it the wrong way? And what was the wrong way anyway? She was in uncharted territory.

His secretary had disappeared. They were alone in his half-acre office, with the view that looked right out over the harbour to the Statue of Liberty. Mary had been in town for twenty-four hours, working up courage to come and see him. She'd queued to climb the Empire State Building to see all over New York.

She needn't have bothered. The view from Logan House was almost the same.

'To what do I owe the pleasure?' he said, and she struggled to get her words in order. She was here for a reason and she needed to get it right.

'I need to thank you.'

'I believe you've already thanked me,' he said gravely. 'Both through my lawyer and through the very nice card you sent me.'

'You make me sound like a ten-year-old writing thank-you notes.'

'I kept the card,' he said. 'I believe I'll always keep the card.'

There was a statement to take her breath away.

He was still holding her hands. Just holding…

'It's me who thanks you, though,' he said. 'You saved my life. I'll owe you forever.'

She gulped. The feel of his hands holding hers was doing strange things. She felt…she felt…

Stop it with the feeling, she told herself. Just say what she needed to say.

'I can't tell you how grateful I was to hear that Jake was safe,' she managed.

'You never doubted it.'

'I never admitted to you that I doubted it.'

He smiled, but his smile didn't reach his eyes. It was a smile that said there was trouble somewhere.

Trouble? What could be wrong in this man's perfect world?

'Is anything wrong?' she asked. 'With Jake, I mean?'

'What should be wrong? He's fine.'

'It's just…you look…'

'He's fine,' he said, almost roughly. But she knew there was something.

How did she know this man so well, this man in his billion-aire's office with his billionaire's suit? She thought, *He has the hawklike, all-seeing eyes but two can play at that game. Reading minds.*

She knew this guy. Inside he was just…Ben.

The thought settled her. It was okay. Underneath the glossy exterior he was still the man she'd held until the terror had faded.

She had been right to come.

'How's Heinz?' he asked.

'Probably bored. My next-door neighbour's looking after him. How's the knee?'

'You came half a world to ask about my knee?'

'No.' It was time. She released his hands and took a step back. She wanted to watch his face when she said what she had to say.

She was here for a purpose. Do it.

'Ben,' she said, and then she paused.

'Mary?'

Say it.

'I came to tell you I'm pregnant.'

CHAPTER EIGHT

HE DIDN'T GET his face right fast enough.

He didn't know how to.

Mary had stepped back so she was standing against the closed doors. She was pressing herself hard against the doors, her chin tilted, almost defiant.

That was an appalling suit she was wearing, he thought irrelevantly. She'd looked better in torn jeans.

Pregnant.

The word seemed to echo round and round the massive office. Deals were done in this room that affected the finances of the world. Yet nothing had ever been said in this office that seemed more important than this.

Pregnant.

'It's okay,' she said, hurriedly now as if she needed to clear whatever it was she saw on his face. 'I'm not here to sue you for half you own. I don't even want acknowledgement if you'd rather not. I just thought…I needed to tell you.'

'But I thought…' He was having trouble getting his voice to work. 'I thought…' But he hadn't thought. That was how it had happened—thought had been shelved. Their mating had been born of primeval need, with no thought of consequences.

The consequences now were blowing his mind.

'Maybe you thought there are morning-after options,' she said. 'There are. I just…didn't think of them until it was way after the morning after.'

And it was all there on her face. This wasn't a discussion about whether or not to go ahead with a pregnancy.

This woman was having his child.

He should walk forward, take her in his arms, hold her close and tell her this was joyful news.

He couldn't.

A baby.

Family.

His mother... The mess that was their family... He'd even messed it up with Jake. He couldn't hold anything together. Could a baby be tough and self-reliant? Not in a million years. But for him to be needed... For a child to rely on him...

'It's okay,' Mary said again, her tone gentling. 'This was a shock to me, too, believe it or not. Sense was blown away with the storm. But now I've decided that I want this baby and, Ben, what you've done for me makes it possible. Thanks to your lawyer I have the cheque from my family and I have my job back. My baby and I will be fine. It's just...I came here because I thought I owed you this much.'

'You owe me?'

'This is not a trap, Ben. I'm not here to ask you for anything. But for me, somehow this pregnancy seems right. I never imagined it but now it's happened it's wondrous. It seems amazing that something like this could come from...from what we had. So the more I thought about it, the more I decided I needed to tell you, face to face, in case for you this baby might help...'

'What on earth do you mean?'

'I mean this baby is bringing me joy, Ben,' she said gently. 'I know there'll be problems. I know it'll be tough, but the moment I realised I was pregnant all I felt was happiness. That something so wonderful could come from such a...'

'Chance coupling?' He said it harshly, cruelly even. She should flinch. Maybe she did, inside, but if she did she hid it well.

'It might have been a chance coupling for you,' she said, the chin tilting again, 'but for me it was like a dividing line. Before and after. I know that doesn't make sense to you but for me it's huge. I went to the island feeling defeated. I came home thinking I could cope with anything the world threw at me. I have the strength and happiness to raise this baby alone. Ben, you have no need to do anything. If you like, I won't even put your name on my baby's birth certificate. But I thought…I just had to tell you.'

He didn't answer. He didn't know what to say.

'I'll go now,' she said gently. 'Ben, there'll be no repercussions. For you it was a chance coupling, but for me it was magic. I believe our baby was conceived in love, and I'll remember that forever. Thank you, Ben. Thank you for my baby. Thank you for everything.'

And she turned and walked out the door.

She'd sounded sure, but her certainty faded the moment she closed the door behind her. Why had she come?

Back in New Zealand it had seemed like the only honourable thing to do. She'd meet him face to face. She'd explain that he was going to be a father.

Okay, a tiny part of her had been hoping for joy, but that was a tiny part. A dumb part.

Mostly she'd thought the conversation would be brief and businesslike, with her assuring him she didn't expect support. He needed to know he had a child but she didn't want more help.

What she hadn't expected was horror.

Maybe he had assumed she was here for a share in the Logan billions, but she didn't think so. The look on Ben's face had said this wasn't about money.

Why wouldn't the elevator come? She shoved the button again and thought maybe she'd hit the fire stairs.

She was a long way up.

She wanted to go home. Fiercely, she wanted to be home.

She never wanted to see that look on Ben's face again. She never wanted her child to see it.

'Mary…'

He was right behind her.

She jabbed the button again.

'I'm sorry,' he said, but she didn't turn around.

'You don't need to be sorry. I've said what I came to say. As far as you're concerned, this is over.'

'When did you arrive?'

'Yesterday.' Jab, jab.

'And when are you going home?'

'Monday.' Jab, jab, jab.

He leaned forward and covered her hand with his, stopping her touching the buttons. His touch seemed to burn.

What was wrong with the stupid elevator? 'You own this building,' she snapped. 'Put in more lifts.'

'Let me take you to lunch.'

'No.'

'That's not very gracious.'

'No!'

'Mary—'

'I've said what I came to say. Let me go.'

'Can I tell you why I reacted…as I did?'

And finally the elevator arrived. All she needed to do was step inside and head for the ground floor. Then catch a cab, collect her gear, head to the airport and go home.

'There's a reason,' he said.

The elevator door closed again and it slid silently away. He put his hands on her shoulders and turned her so she was facing him.

'Tell me.' She felt weary beyond belief. Jet-lag? Early pregnancy? She'd been feeling the effects of both these things but the look on Ben's face had made them ten times worse.

'I can't…' he said.

'Tell me,' she repeated, and she thought tears weren't far off. But why should she cry now? She'd had this sorted, or she'd thought she had.

Until she'd seen the fear.

'I don't do families,' he said.

This was a dumb place to have such a conversation, she thought inconsequentially. Outside the elevators. Public.

And then she glanced over Ben's shoulder and realised the palatial reception area was designed for one secretary and Elsbeth was nowhere to be seen. This whole floor was Ben's.

This was Ben's world and she had no place here. But…was this his refuge as Hideaway Island had been hers?

A storm had destroyed her refuge. Was she threatening his?

She wasn't. He didn't do families? She wasn't asking that of him.

But it seemed he intended to tell.

'Mary, my father, his father and his father before him practically owned Manhattan,' he said. 'My father was a womanising megalomaniac. My mother was a talented, beautiful, fragile screen star. Rita Marlene. You may have heard of her. She needed support and love and appreciation to thrive and with my father she got nothing.

'After Jake and I were born she retreated into her stage world, where her only reality was her acting. It reached the point where even when she was upset, we never knew what was real or make-believe. Ophelia, Lady Macbeth, Anna Karenina, Jake and I had them all. Plus isolation and nannies. The only time Jake and I were noticed by our parents was when we did something outrageous and, believe me, we made outrageous a life skill.

'I don't think we realised…how much worse it made everything. That every time we hit trouble our father blamed Rita. Rita.' He gave a harsh, short laugh. 'She was always Rita. Stage Rita. Never Mom. And my father was Sir.'

'Ben—'

'I know, this is self-indulgent history,' he said harshly. 'But hear me out. When we were fourteen Jake and I stole a car. Not just any car either,' he said, and once again there was an attempt at a smile. 'My father was trying to stitch up a deal with a spoiled brat son-of-a-sheikh. An oil magnate. He had him to stay in our family mansion and pulled out all stops to impress.

'You can imagine the scene. Servants everywhere, my mother dressed up in the most beautiful ballgown, almost ethereal, playing the subservient wife to a T. I believe…' He hesitated. 'I think now she was heavily into drugs. All the signs were there only, of course, no one wanted to see.'

'Oh, Ben…'

But he wasn't stopping. He knew she'd seen the horror, and maybe he had to explain.

'And so my father was barking orders, desperate to impress, bullying the servants, bullying Rita. And Jake and I were ordered to dress in suits we hated and present ourselves in the drawing room to be introduced as his sons. It did his street cred good,' he added. 'To have fine sons who obeyed every order.'

She didn't know where this was going. She thought she didn't want to.

'Only then my mother spilled her drink,' he said. 'She was sitting right beside the son-of-sheikh. He was looking at her in a way Jake and I hated, and she spilled it. And my father walked over, wrenched her to her feet and told her to get out. Apologies, apologies, apologies. And then I called him a….' And he said a word that made her cringe.

'Ben…'

'So that was it. We were propelled out, too. My father's pride was to be protected at all costs. The last thing we heard was my father apologising for his stupid family, and the son-of-a-sheikh agreeing that women and children were an eternal problem.'

She could hardly breathe. She didn't want to know, and yet… 'And so?' she managed.

'So Jake and I went out and hot-wired the son-of-a-sheikh's Lamborghini. Jake drove it all the way to Soho and then crashed it into the rear of a stationary bus. Jake swears the bus jumped out to greet us. Jake was concussed and taken to hospital and I spent the night in jail, not knowing if Jake was alive or dead. There was no way my father would bail me out that night. My father's assistant finally came to get me. I returned home the next morning to find my father apoplectic and my mother with a black eye and hysterical.'

'Oh, Ben…'

'His pride had been hurt—of course it had—so he'd taken it

out on her. And she kept crying and crying, and saying, "Sorry, Ben, sorry. My babies… Ben, you take care of Jake. He's your responsibility now." I thought she was talking about the crash, about Jake getting hurt. She was so melodramatic. To my never-ending regret I remember thinking, *Who are you playing now?*

'The hysterics went on and on. It was so real it terrified me but finally there was silence. My father went out. Jake was still in hospital. I was scared for Rita, but I was still scared for Jake. I lay in bed that night and told myself of course she was acting. I was angry, too. Jail had been shocking. I'd been terrified. Why hadn't Rita stood up to him? Why wasn't she stronger? Why wouldn't she tell me how Jake was? So I should have gone to her and I didn't. But she wasn't acting. She overdosed and was dead before morning.'

Mary didn't move. She couldn't. She thought of her own lonely childhood and she thought…how could it possibly compare? What had been placed on this man's shoulders… His mother's death.

'You were fourteen,' she said gently. 'You didn't know.'

'I should have.'

'And Jake…'

'You think I told him any of this? The black eye? The blame? He thought Mom died of an accidental overdose. How could I lay any more on him?'

'He still doesn't know?'

'The last minutes in the yacht,' he said heavily, 'I threw it at him. He was playing the martyr, telling me to go first. He has a weak leg, courtesy of the Afghanistan injury. I told him to get into the harness or he'd be suiciding, just like Rita. It shocked him enough to get into the harness, to get him to safety. But now…'

'He's holding it against you?'

'Who knows what Jake's thinking? He's certainly talking to me in words of one syllable. "Yes." "No." "I can't talk." "Bye."'

'And you?' she said gently. 'Where does that leave you?'

'Not with a family,' he said bluntly. 'Jake takes after Rita. He retreats into his acting world. Reality blurs. For me, though, try as I may, I'm my father's son. I enjoy running this company. I enjoy control. But all my life…' He took a deep breath. 'Ever since my mother died I've avoided the personal. One night, one vicious outburst and my father destroyed our family. Rita told me I was responsible for Jake. After she died I swore I'd never be responsible for anyone else.'

And she got it. She could read it on his face. 'You think you might end up like your father, too?'

'I'll never put myself in the position to find out.'

'No one's asking you to.'

'You're asking me to be a father.'

'No. I've given you the opt-out clause, remember?'

'How can I opt out?'

'Easy,' she said, and somehow she found the strength to drum up a smile. 'You can smile at me, say congratulations, wish me all the best and say goodbye.'

There was a long silence. He looked at her, he simply looked, and when he nodded she knew that somehow he'd moved on.

'I'll give you lunch first.'

'I'll accept lunch,' she said, still smiling determinedly. 'But nothing else. I'm no risk to your world, Ben, and neither is our baby. You're still free to be…as free as you wish. You're not responsible for our baby.'

Our baby.

The two words stayed with him as they left the building, but they weren't small. They echoed over and over in his head, like a drumbeat, like an off-rhythm metronome.

Like a nightmare.

He couldn't be a father. How could he risk…?

It'd been his stupid idea to steal the Lamborghini. The consequences had stayed with him all his life. His mother had died because of his stupidity.

His father had been a gross bully. He'd battered his wife but he hadn't killed her. *He* had done that by ignoring her, by not reading the difference between real and fantasy.

He'd spent his life trying not to tell Jake, trying to pretend it had never happened, being responsible. But one revelation from a slip of a girl and he'd told her everything.

Why? She wasn't asking him to commit to any part of this baby's life. There'd been no reason to spill his guts, and yet…the look on her face… To turn away from her was like slapping her.

He could do financial support. He decided that as they reached the ground floor. He'd be in the States. She'd be in New Zealand. There was no reason for him ever needing to see his…the child.

When…it…turned eighteen…it…might want to meet him. That could be okay.

'You're putting a note in your mental diary to have dinner when he turns twenty-one,' Mary said, and he turned and stared down at her. They were in the foyer. His colleagues, his staff were casting curious looks at the woman by his side.

The mother of his baby?

What was it with this woman? How could she read his mind?

'How did you know what I was thinking?'

'You're like an open book.'

'I'm not. And I wasn't thinking his twenty-first. It was his eighteenth.' Deep breath. 'Do we know if it's a he?'

'I don't have a clue,' she said cheerfully. 'Does it matter?'

'Of course not.

But then he thought, *A son.*

And then he thought, *A daughter.*

'You're getting that hunted look again,' she told him. 'You needn't worry. If you turn into your father, I'll be between you and our child with a blunderbuss.'

'I believe that,' he said. 'I've watched you playing roller derby.'

It was her turn to stare. 'Where?'

'YouTube.'

'You watched me?'

'Last year's finals. A woman who plays like that…who looks like that… I wouldn't get in her way for the world.'

'There you are, then. You don't have to worry about being like your father. I'll put on full make-up and intervene.'

'Don't,' he said, suddenly savage.

'Don't?'

'Put on make-up. Pretend. Jake does it all the time. My mother did it. They move into their acting world and disappear.'

'Is that what Jake's done now? Is that why you're hurting?'

'Can we quit it with the inquisition?' It was a savage demand but she didn't flinch.

'Sorry.' She sounded almost cheerful. They'd negotiated the revolving doors and were out in the weak spring sunshine. New York was doing its best to impress.

Where to take her for lunch?

Clive's was his normal business option, with comfortable seating, discreet booths, excellent food and an air of muted elegance. Clive himself always greeted him and no matter how busy, a booth was always assured.

He took Mary's arm and steered her Clive-wards, but she dug in her heels.

'The park's thataway, right?'

'Yes, but—'

'And it's Central Park. That's where the Imagine garden is. Strawberry Fields Forever. I loved John Lennon. Can we buy a sandwich and go there?'

'It'll be full of—'

'Kids and dogs,' she finished for him. 'Exactly. My kind of place.'

'I guess it will be if you have this baby.'

'It is anyway,' she said, her voice gentling, as if she needed to reassure him. 'I'm a district nurse. Kids and mums and oldies are what I do. Along with grass under my feet. Ben, I'm still jet-lagged. Fresh air will do me good.'

Now that she mentioned it, she was looking pale. He should have noticed before, but she was wearing drab clothes, she looked incredibly different from the last time he'd seen her and the news she'd brought had been shocking. Now he took the time to look more closely.

'You've been ill.'

'Morning sickness,' she said darkly. 'Only they lie. Morning... Ha!'

'But you decided to fly to New York, morning sickness and all.'

'It didn't seem right not to tell you.'

'Telephone?'

'I wanted to watch your face when I said it.'

'So you've said it. And I've been found wanting.'

'You haven't,' she said, and tucked her arm into his. 'You've explained why you're afraid of being a father. If I'd telephoned I'd never have got that. I'd have raised Gertrude or Archibald to think Dad doesn't care, rather than Dad cares too much. Where can we get a sandwich?'

Dad. The word did his head in.

'If we're having a sandwich we're having the very best sandwich,' he growled, fighting an emotion he didn't know how to handle.

'Excellent. Lead the way. We're right beside you.'

We.

Discombobulated didn't begin to describe how he felt.

CHAPTER NINE

HE HAD A diary packed with meetings.

He sat on the grass and ate sandwiches and drank soda with the mother of his child.

It seemed she'd done what she'd come to do. As far as Mary was concerned, the baby conversation was over. She chatted about the devastation caused by Cyclone Lila, about the rebuilding efforts, about Barbara and Henry's dejection at the possibility of selling a cyclone-ravaged island.

'Maybe I can buy it,' Ben found himself saying.

'Why on earth would you?' She'd hardly touched her sandwich, he noted. When she thought he wasn't watching she broke bits off and stuffed them into her bag.

Just how bad was the morning sickness?

'Because I can?'

'Just how rich are you?'

'Too rich for my own good,' he said, and grinned. 'It's a problem.'

'Where's your dad?'

'He died ten years ago. Heart attack. It couldn't have happened to a nicer man.'

'You really hated him.'

'Yes,' he said. 'I did. He was a total controller. Jake and I were supposed to go straight into the business. The power he wielded... We went into the army to get away from it. There was another dumb decision. It was only when he died that I took the first forays into commerce and found I loved it.'

'It doesn't mean you're like him.'

'No.' His voice told her not to go there, and she respected it. She abandoned her sandwich, lay back on the grass and looked up through the trees.

'It's the same here as in New Zealand,' she said in satisfaction. 'Trees. Grass. Sky. Nice.'

'You'd never want to live here.'

'No.'

He looked down at her. She'd come all the way from New Zealand to tell him something that could have been said over the phone. He'd reacted just about as badly as it was possible to react. She was in a strange country, she was jet-lagged and she was morning sick.

She looked happy?

'What?' she said, seeing his confusion.

'You could be a bit angry.'

'What's to be angry about?'

'If you had a half-decent dad he'd be here with a shotgun. I'd be being marched down the aisle and we'd be living happily ever after.'

'I don't see shotgun weddings leading to happy ever after.'

'But you're happy without it.'

'I'll have a job I love, my roller-derby team, a baby I think I'll adore to bits, enough money to exist on and trees, grass, sky. Oh, and Heinz. What more could a woman want?'

She was so…brave. He had so many emotions running through his head he didn't know how to handle them, but he looked down at her and he thought, involved or not, he wanted to help. Despite her protestations, he knew how hard the life she'd chosen would be, and the thought of this woman facing it alone was doing his head in.

'Mary, you won't have just enough money to exist,' he growled. 'You're having my child. I'll buy you a decent house; set you up with everything you need. You needn't go back to work.'

She thought about that for a bit.

He wanted to lie beside her. He was wearing an Armani suit. The grass…

'The grass is comfy,' she said.

And he thought, *What the hell,* and lay beside her.

She was gazing up through the treetops. The sky was amazingly blue. The tree was vast. He felt…small.

His body was touching hers. She was so close. He wanted…

'Just enough for the baby,' she said.

And he thought, *What?* What had they been talking about?

'The money,' she said, as if she'd heard his unspoken question. 'I don't want anything for me, but it'd be nice to think if he or she wants to go to university the choice won't be dictated by my finances. You're the dad. Our kid'll be smart.'

She said it like she was pleased. Like she'd made a good decision to choose him to father his child.

He sat up again. 'Mary…'

And once again she got what he was thinking. 'I did not plan this,' she said evenly.

'How do I know?'

'What, lie on an island and wait for a stud to be washed up? Hope to be pregnant? Why?'

'I have no idea.'

'You also have no idea how this pregnancy will affect my family,' she said, in that soft, even voice that he was growing to trust. 'They'll hate me. They've been forced to back down in their accusations. Now I'll turn up pregnant when my sister's just lost her baby. They'll tell me I'm rubbing their faces in it. It'll hurt. This isn't all roses, Ben.'

'But did you want it?'

'No,' she said, and she said it in such a way that he believed her. 'To be honest, I've avoided relationships. My father's…desertion gutted me, and I've always thought if I can't trust my dad, who can I trust? Like you, my family background doesn't leave me aching to copy it. But now…maybe you're right in one sense. Even though I didn't set you up, I'm welcoming this baby. Somehow the night of the storm changed things for me. I do want it.'

'Despite you not being in a position to afford it.'

'I can afford it. I didn't come here for money. Set up a trust or something for the baby if you want, but I want nothing.'

Nothing.

He thought of all he had here. A financial empire. An apartment overlooking Central Park. Any material thing he could possibly desire.

What would happen if he lost everything?

He'd have trees, grass, sky. Right now they felt okay.

It might get draughty in winter, he conceded, and he looked at Mary and he thought she'd just build a willow cabin or find a cave. She was a survivor and she didn't complain. She'd care for this baby.

And suddenly he felt…jealous? That was weird, he conceded, but there it was. He was jealous of an unborn child—because it'd have a mother like Mary.

'How's the book going?' he asked, feeling disoriented, trying to get things back on track, though he wasn't sure where the track was.

He saw her flinch.

'You don't have to tell me.'

She thought about it. 'That's okay,' she conceded. 'Maybe I have to open up a bit there, too. It's always been my private escape, my writing. If I'm to have this baby then I need to share.'

'So…share?' The request felt huge, he thought. It was only about a book, he reminded himself. Nothing else. 'Is it proceeding?' he asked.

'It is.' He could see her make a conscious effort to relax. 'In your fictional life you've been drinking weird, smoky cocktails with three slutty sisters, squeezing them for information, and all of a sudden they've transformed themselves into dragons. Very gruesome it is, and rather hot, but you're handling yourself nicely.'

'A true hero?'

'You'd better believe it.'

'Will you try for publication?'

'A million authors are striving for publication. What makes you think anyone would like my book?'

'I like it.'

'That's 'cos you're the hero. I'll send you a copy when I've worked out my happy ever after.'

'Happy ever after works in books?'

'You have to believe in it somewhere.'

A cloud drifted over the sun. A shadow crossed Mary's face and she shivered. Enough. He rose and put down a hand to help her up.

She stared at it for a moment as if she was considering whether to take it. Whether she should.

'You need to let me help a little,' he said gently. 'I'd like to.'

'I'd like to help, too,' she said. 'Where's Jake?'

'Still in New Zealand, winding up his movie.'

'Would you like me to talk to him?'

'No.'

'That's not very polite.'

'Families are complicated.

'You don't need to tell me that.' She ignored his hand and pushed herself to her feet, wincing a little as she did.

'You're hurt?' The tiny flash of pain did something to him. She was pregnant. What did he know about pregnancy? Surely she shouldn't have flown. What if there were complications? What if…?

'Twenty-four hours squashed in a tin can is enough to make anyone achy,' she said. 'So let's get that "Call the artillery and have me carted off to Emergency" look off your face.'

'Am I that obvious?'

'Yes.'

'You're sure you're okay?'

'Yes.'

'Where are you staying?'

She told him and he struggled to keep his face still. Not a salubrious district. Cheap.

This was the mother of his child.

No. This was Mary.

'I'll take you home,' he said.

'I've just figured out the subway.'

'Good for you but I'll still take you home.'

'You have a car?'

He hauled out his cellphone. 'James will be here in two minutes.'

'Wow,' she whispered. 'Wow, wow, wow. Bring on James.'

She sat in the back of a car that'd have everybody back home gathered round and staring. She sat beside Ben, and a chauffeur called James drove her back to her hotel.

It wasn't in a salubrious part of town. It wasn't a salubrious hotel.

The chauffeur pulled to a halt out the front of the less-than-five-star establishment and turned to Ben.

'Is this the right address, sir?'

'No,' Ben said. 'It's not.' He turned to Mary. 'When did you arrive?'

'The day before yesterday?'

'You've stayed here for two nights?' His tone was incredulous.

'It's clean,' she said. 'I checked it out on the internet before coming. It has everything I need and it's near the subway.'

'It doesn't have everything I need. This is a dodgy neighbourhood at the best of times. I bet you've been walking around alone, too. It's a miracle you weren't mugged.'

'I can look after myself.'

'Not if you're staying here you can't.' He sighed. 'James, stay with the car. Do not under any circumstances leave it alone in this district. We'll be as fast as possible.'

'We?' Mary pushed open the car door. 'There's no we. You've brought me home. Thank you very much. Goodbye.'

'You're not staying here.'

'Says you and whose army?'

'I am,' he said through gritted teeth, 'a trained commando. I'll take you by force if necessary.'

'Oooooh,' she said, pretending to cower. And then she sighed. 'Quit it with the dramatics. Bye, Ben.' She was out of the car and up the steps of the hotel—but he was right beside her.

'I said goodbye,' she hissed.

'I heard. Let me see inside.'

'No.'

'It's a public hotel.'

'No!'

'You're the mother of my baby,' he said, loudly, possessively, and she stopped and stared.

'My baby?'

'That's why you came all the way to New York. To tell me I have a share in this. I might not be able to dictate where you stay but I will have a say in how safe our child is.'

She stared at him.

She hadn't thought this through, she decided. Had she given him the right to dictate how she treated…his child?

What had she done?

'It's fine,' she said through gritted teeth, and he took her arm and smiled down at her, and she knew that smile. It was his *I'm in charge and you'd better come along quietly or I'll turn into a Logan* smile.

'Let's just see, shall we?'

Which explained why twenty minutes later she was standing on the doorstep of what must be one of the most awesome apartments in Manhattan, staring around with shocked amazement.

'I can't stay here!'

He hadn't quite picked her up and carried her but he might as well have. One look at her dreary hotel room, with its window that looked at a brick wall, with the smell of the downstairs hamburger joint drifting through the window and a bathroom with mould, and the father of her child had simply gathered her possessions and led her out. All the way to his place.

'I have plenty of room,' he said, dumping her decidedly downmarket duffel on the floor of his breathtaking apartment. She could see her face in the marble floor tiles. Her duffel was travel-stained and old. It looked ridiculous sitting against such opulence.

'My father bought this as his alternative to home when Rita's histrionics got too much,' he said briefly. 'Five bedrooms. My father never did things small.'

'N-no.' She crossed to the wall of French windows leading to the balcony. Leading to Central Park.

She needn't have bothered asking to have her picnic there. She could see the Lennon garden from here.

'It's convenient,' he told her. 'You'll be able to sightsee until you go home.'

'I should go home now.'

'But your flight isn't until Monday.'

'I… Yes.' Her last-minute decision to come here and tell him had meant last-minute tickets. Which meant not the weekend. Today was Friday. She'd have two days living in this… this…place.

'It's scary,' she said, staring around at the cool, grey and white marble, the kitchen that boasted four ovens, the massive leather lounge suites, the tinkling waterfall behind the living room wall. 'It scares me to death.'

'It beats the cave on Hideaway.'

'On Hideaway we had cushions and Barbara's quilt. Comfy. How do you get comfy here?'

'I'm not here much.'

'Social life?'

'I work.' He crossed to the kitchen, opened the massive fridge and stared into its interior as if he didn't know what the contents were but knew he'd find something.

'Soda? Cheese and crackers? Cold chicken?'

'I've just had lunch. Who fills your refrigerator?'

'A housekeeping service.'

'A housekeeper?'

'It's a service. More convenient than just the one employee. I don't need to worry about holidays.'

'So you don't even need to know your housekeeper.'

'They come and go when I'm not here.'

'That's awful.'

'What's awful about it?'

'You really are alone.'

'I don't need anyone,' he told her. 'I like my life.'

'You need Jake.'

A shadow crossed his face then. How had this woman guessed what was hurting him?

He didn't want to talk about it but then…this was Mary. Maybe he did.

'We fight to be independent,' he told her. 'But the twin thing makes it harder. When he was hurt in Afghanistan I damned near died myself. And when I didn't know whether that chopper had made it…it's not a sensation I'd like to repeat.'

'So you don't want to get close to anyone else?'

'I don't want the responsibility of loving like that—but I will do the right thing by your baby.'

'You just said it was our baby.'

'It is,' he said, and he sounded strained. 'So I will do what I can.'

'I hope he's grateful.' She gazed around with distaste. 'I can tell you one thing, though. If he's any child of mine, he won't want to inherit this place.'

Inherit. The word was a biggie. Why had she said it? It took things to a whole new level.

She watched Ben's face change again.

'I didn't mean…' She spoke too fast, trying to take things back. 'Ben, I'm not expecting anything, I told you. This baby… if you want, he can be brought up not even knowing he's your son. Or daughter for that matter. Inheritance is nonsense. We won't interfere with your life.'

'You already have interfered.'

'I shouldn't have told you?'

'Of course you should.' He raked his hair in that gesture she was starting to know. It softened him, she thought. It took away the image of businessman Ben and gave her back the image of Ben in a cave. The Ben she needed to care for.

'Ben, you like your isolation,' she said softly. 'We're not threatening that. I'll return to New Zealand and ask nothing of you. If you want, you can set up a trust for this child's education, but I'll not raise him expecting anything from you. You can walk away.'

'I can't walk away.'

'But I can,' she said. 'And I will. Come Monday. Meanwhile, which of these doors leads to a bedroom I can use?'

'The bedroom at the end of the hall's mine. Choose any other. They all have en suites.'

'Of course.'

'Mary?'

'Yes?'

'Have a nap,' he told her. 'Then I'll take you out to dinner.'

'I'm having a sleep, not a nap,' she told him. 'A really long one. I'm jet-lagged like you wouldn't believe and this pregnancy makes me want to sleep all the time. You can go back to whatever you were doing. You need to be independent and I'm not messing with that. Thank you, Ben, and goodnight.'

She slept. He headed for his study and stared out over the park.

He needed time to work out all that was inside him.

Maybe it wasn't possible for him to work it out.

Mary was carrying his child. He was going to be a father.

Coming, ready or not.

The old chant, sung by children for ages past in the game of hide and seek, was suddenly echoing around in his head, almost as a taunt.

A father.

Abortion? The word drifted through his consciousness but

when he tried to work out some way he could say it to her, something like a wall rose up.

He couldn't say it.

He didn't want to say it.

This would be Mary's baby and he didn't want her not to have a child. It was a convoluted thought but it was there as a certainty. And somehow... The time in the cave with her had been time out, like a watershed, where fear had laid all bare. That a child should come of it... It seemed okay.

Was that sentiment? Was it hope?

He couldn't get his head around it.

He didn't have to, he told himself. For some reason Mary had come halfway around the world to tell him, yet she was proposing leaving again on Monday. He never needed to see her again. He could pay into a trust account once a month. He could stop thinking about it.

How could he stop thinking about it? He slammed his fist down on the desk so hard it hurt, and suddenly he wished he could talk to Jake. Ring him. 'Jake, I've screwed up...'

In his present mood Jake could well say he should tell someone who cared.

In this position Jake might do better, he conceded. Jake would be able to play the caring dad. He was great at acting.

If he himself was better at acting, maybe he could pull this off.

Pull what off? Being a caring dad?

He couldn't do it. He didn't know how. He thought back to the rages and the coldness that had been his childhood. He tried to think how he could possibly relate to a child.

He could try, but he couldn't act, and if he felt nothing...

His father had felt nothing. His mother...she'd told them she'd loved them but in different ways all the time. Like she was playing different roles.

'I won't act,' he told himself. 'I can only do what I can do, and I won't put myself in a position of power.'

So what could he do? Send money? That felt so much

like what his father would do. Send money and get rid of the problem.

On impulse he hit the internet, heading for the site where Smash 'em Mary flew round the track, dodging and weaving, leading her team to victory.

It was a rough game, and that was putting it mildly.

Surely she wouldn't be able to play now she was pregnant.

The words of the lawyer he'd sent to help her echoed in his ears as well.

'We've won her monetary compensation, and she's been re-instated in her position as district nurse, but there is local antag-onism,' he'd told him. 'Her father and stepmother are wealthy. They control much of the commerce in the town and people are afraid to upset them. Her stepmother is vindictive, more so now that we've forced this resolution. Life's not going to be easy for your Mary.'

Your Mary. The words had swept over him then, but they came back to haunt him now.

She wasn't His Mary. She was a woman he scarcely knew. He'd been stranded with her for two days. Two days was tiny.

She was a woman who'd come half a world to tell him she was pregnant because it was the right thing to do.

His fist slammed on the desk again. Lucky the walls were solid. Lucky Mary was sleeping three bedrooms away.

He needed to get away. Think. Go back to the office? Do something to stop him going mad.

He headed back to the living room. He'd carried Mary's duf-fel into her bedroom for her but her capacious purse was still on the bench. It looked shabby, worn, and it pricked his conscience as nothing else could.

A folder was edging out the top.

And suddenly he was back at the cave, waiting for Mary to come back from her interminable search of the island, hating himself that he couldn't be with her. Distracting himself by reading Mary's make-believe. He'd been the hero.

'I wonder what I've done now?' he said aloud, and looked at the purse again.

She knew he'd read the beginning. It was sitting on the bench, an open invitation. She'd said he was facing dragons.

He could just...read.

But not here. The proximity to Mary—to a woman he hardly knew, he reminded himself—was doing his head in.

He lifted the folder from her purse and put it in his briefcase.

He'd just go...somewhere and disappear into Mary's fictional world.

Maybe Jake was right. Maybe reality had too much to answer for.

CHAPTER TEN

SHE WOKE AT MIDNIGHT, thirsty beyond measure, and also hungry. She woke regretting those nibbled lunchtime sandwiches.

She headed out to the kitchen. The apartment was in darkness—or maybe not. Back in New Zealand the darkness at night was absolute. Here, the lights of the city glimmered through the drapes. Glamorous footlights were placed strategically around the skirting boards so no one could lose their way at night. There was a light on in the sitting room.

She was in New York. More, she was in Ben's fabulous apartment. Marble, glass, discreet lighting, floor-to-ceiling windows overlooking Central Park…

Money plus.

Her inheritance gaffe was still smarting. 'I never should have come,' she muttered to herself. 'Of course he'll think I'm after his money.'

But it had seemed wrong not to. She'd needed to tell him and for some reason she'd felt she had to do it soon. Before the time had come where she could terminate?

Not that she'd considered terminating. She wasn't sure why this little life was so precious, why she'd discovered she was pregnant and felt joy rather than dismay, but she had.

'And maybe I sort of wanted Ben to feel that way, too,' she muttered.

'Feel what way?'

He was on a window seat in the sitting room, working on his laptop. Wearing a bathrobe. Silk. She was in a T-shirt and jogging pants.

She felt like a poor relation.

He looked…hot.

Put it aside, she told herself, and somehow she stopped looking at him. It took an effort.

'I'm hungry,' she said, heading for the kitchen. She hauled open the massive refrigerator doors and thought, *Whoa...* 'How many people live here?'

'My housekeeper caters for every eventuality.'

Yep, money.

Get over it, she told herself. 'I just need toast.'

'I'll make it for you.'

'I can do it. Go back to bed.'

'I don't sleep much,' he said.

'It's a biggie.' She was staring into the refrigerator, thinking all sorts of things—like how hot he looked with his silk bathrobe open and…and forcing herself to think of condiments. Three types of jam. No, make that four. The raspberry looked good, but then there was quince…

'What's a biggie?'

Deep breath. The conversation couldn't all be about jam, and it surely couldn't be about silk bathrobes. 'Learning you're about to be a dad.'

He walked over and set about making toast while she went back to deciding on condiments. Tricky.

She was so aware of his body.

The island bench—approximately a mile long—gave her a couple of yards' clearance from Ben. She hauled herself up on the bench to watch toast-making.

'Most people sit on the stools,' Ben said mildly.

She peered behind the bench to see a row of fancy designer stools. Chrome and leather. Four different colours. Or make that shades. Designers did shades.

'How could I choose which one to sit on?' she demanded. 'I had enough trouble with jam.'

'You want tea?'

'No, thanks.' Actually, she would like tea but it'd mean she had to stay out here for longer. With this body.

Um…Ben. His name was Ben.

Maybe she should start calling him Mr Logan.

'I've been thinking I'm glad you don't want a termination,' he said.

She stilled. He was watching the toast. She was watching the breadth of his back. To all intents and purposes they were a couple talking cosy domestic things—like termination.

'Why?' she managed, and he abandoned the toast and turned to face her.

'It's been a shock,' he said softly. 'All afternoon…all tonight. Heaven knows how you slept but I couldn't. I wouldn't have wished for it but now it's happened…I do want this child.'

And he said it so fiercely that it was lucky she'd put the jam down.

There was a lot to think about in that statement. A lot to make her heart falter.

'One part of me's pleased to hear you say that,' she admitted at last. 'I was never going to terminate, not for a moment, but in a way I think that's why I came here so early in the pregnancy. I needed to know your reaction. I wanted my choice to be your choice.'

'But the other part?'

Say it like it is, she decided. Just say it. 'Another part of me almost had a heart attack, just this minute,' she admitted. 'Do you want this child like you want another Logan? And how much do you want it? Enough to sue me for custody? I hadn't even thought about that.'

'I would never do that to you. And she's your baby.'

'She?'

'I thought tonight…' He looked at her for a long moment, his expression unreadable, but when he spoke, it was all tenderness. 'I thought, what if she's a girl, just like her mother?'

What was there in that statement to take her breath away? What was there in that statement to make her forget toast and jam, to forget where she was, to forget everything except those words?

What if she's a girl, just like her mother?

She'd been terrific when she'd found out she was pregnant, she'd decided. She'd surprised herself by how calm she'd been. She'd set about making plans, figuring how she could manage.

She'd decided to tell Ben, rationally and coolly. She'd prided herself on her efficiency, getting a passport, deciding on flights, choosing the hotel Ben had so rudely rejected.

She'd told him calmly. Everything was going as planned.

But one little statement…

What if she's a girl, just like her mother?

She sat on the bench and stared, and suddenly the cool control she'd kept herself under for the last couple of months snapped.

She couldn't help it. Tears were rolling down her cheeks and there wasn't a thing she could do about it. She couldn't speak. She just sat there and cried like a baby.

Ben looked like he didn't have a clue how to handle it. That made two of them.

'Mary, I didn't mean…' He sounded appalled. 'Mary, stop.'

That'd be like asking the tide to turn. She gave her tears an angry swipe but nothing could stop these suckers.

She didn't have a tissue. She didn't have thirty tissues. Where were tissues in this über-rich mausoleum of a marble apartment?

One minute he was standing by the kitchen bench, talking to a woman he'd decided he hardly knew. The next moment the woman had turned into Mary. *His Mary.*

He knew this woman like he knew himself.

Tears were rolling down her cheeks and she was making no effort to check them. It was as if she didn't know what to do with them.

This was a woman who seldom cried. He knew that. What was happening now was shocking her—as well as shocking him.

She needed tissues, but his shoulder was closer. He stepped forward, gathered a sodden Mary into his arms and held her.

He should wear a towelling robe, he thought ruefully. Silk didn't cut it with tears.

Silk didn't cut it when the feel of her body was soaking through. But he held her and held her, until the shuddering eased, until she'd cried herself out, until he felt the imperceptible stiffening that told him she'd realised what she'd done, where she was.

He still held. He was cradling her like a child but this was no child. She'd slumped against him but the slump had turned to something more. Her face was buried in his shoulder but the rest of her... She was moulded to him. Her breasts were pressed to his chest. His face was in her hair.

'I can't...' It was a ragged whisper.

'I have it in hand,' he told her, and before she could make any objections he swung her into his arms and strode with her into his bedroom.

The woman needed tissues. There were tissues in his bedroom and that's where he was headed.

One minute she was cradled against Ben Logan, sobbing her heart out, releasing months of pent-up emotion and who knew what else besides. The next she was in his arms, being carried into his bedroom.

She should make some sort of protest, but who was protesting? She was making no protest at all.

They'd made love before as complete strangers. They weren't strangers now. Or maybe they were, she thought, dazed. How did she know this man?

She did.

He lived in a different world from her, a world he pretty much owned.

She felt she knew him inside out.

To the world this man was a hero, a rich, smart, controlling wheeler and dealer in the world's finances. But she'd seen what lay beneath. She'd seen the core that was pure need.

Who was she kidding? The need was entirely hers and she couldn't resist it for a minute.

She was catching her breath, finding control of a sort. The dumb weeping had stopped so when Ben set her on the bathroom bench and handed her a wad of tissues she could do something about it.

She blew her nose, hard, and Ben blinked.

'There's my romantic girl.'

She choked on something between a chuckle and a sob, but it was erring more towards the chuckle.

Something was happening inside her. She was in this man's bathroom. He was looking at her with such concern...

'Your face is puffy.'

'And there's a truly romantic statement,' she managed. 'I bet you say that to all the women in your life.'

'There are no women in my life.' He picked up a facecloth, wet it and gently wiped her eyes. Then her whole face. 'Just the mother of my child.'

What was it about that statement that took her breath away? That made her toes curl?

That made her drop her tissues into the neat designer trash slot and look up at him and smile.

'Ben...'

It was all she had to say. All the longing in the world was in that word. It was a question and an answer all by itself.

She put her arms up and looped her hands around his neck. He stopped and lifted her yet again.

'Your place or mine?' he asked huskily, managing to smile.

'I've only got a king-size bed,' she managed back. 'Puny. I bet yours is bigger.'

'You'd better believe it,' he said, and she did.

And that was practically the last thing she was capable of thinking for a very long time.

She woke and the morning sun was streaming over the luxurious white coverlet. She woke and the softness of the duvet enfolded her.

She woke and Ben was gone.

For a moment she refused to let herself think it. She lay and savoured the warmth, the feeling of sheer, unmitigated luxury, the knowledge that she'd been made love to with a passion that maybe she'd never feel again.

He'd made her feel alive. He'd made her feel a woman as she'd never believed she could feel.

He'd made her feel loved.

But he wasn't here now.

She'd slept, at last, cocooned in the strength and heat of his body. She'd slept thinking everything was right in her world. What could possibly be wrong?

She'd slept thinking she was being held by Ben and he'd never let her go.

She stirred, tentatively, like a caterpillar nervous of emerging from the safety of its dreamlike cocoon.

The clock on her bedside table said twelve.

Twelve? She'd slept how long? No wonder Ben had left her. He'd left her.

Hey, she was still in his bed. Possession's nine tenths of the law, she decided, and stretched like a languorous cat.

Cat, caterpillar, whatever. She surely wasn't herself.

There was a note on his pillow.

A Dear John letter? She almost smiled. She was playing make-believe in her head. Scenario after scenario. All of them included Ben.

The note, however, was straightforward. Not a lot of room for fantasy here.

I need to go into work. I left loose ends yesterday and they're getting strident. Sleep as long as you want. It's Saturday, no cleaners come near the place so you have the apartment to yourself. I'll be home late but tomorrow is yours. Think of what you'd like to do with it.
Ben.

And then a postscript.

Last night was amazing. Please make yourself at home in my bed.

There was more stuff to think about.

She was interrupting his life, she thought. She really had pulled him out of his world yesterday. He'd need to pull it back together.

And then come back to her?

Just for tomorrow.

'But if that's all I can have, then that has to be enough,' she told herself. 'So think about it.'

Food first. What had happened to last night's toast? Who could remember? But she'd seen juice in the fridge, and croissants. And then…the bath in Ben's bathroom was big enough to hold a small whale.

'Which is what I'll be in six months…

'Don't think about it. Don't think about anything but tomorrow,' she said severely. 'Or maybe not even tomorrow. Let's just concentrate on right now.'

The office was chaos. One day out and the sky had fallen. Still, it had been worth it, he decided, making one apologetic phone call after another, trying to draw together the threads of the deal he'd abandoned the day before.

Mary was worth it.

She was with him all day, her image, the memory of her body against his, the warmth of her smile, the taste of her tears.

He was getting soft in his old age. He'd vowed never to feel this way about a woman.

About anyone.

He didn't want to feel responsible for anyone but somehow it had happened. Ready or not, he was responsible for Mary. The mother of his child.

His woman?

He wanted to phone Jake.

Why? To tell him he'd met someone? Jake's attitude to

women was the same as his. His brother had made one foray into marriage and it'd turned into a disaster. The woman had needed far more than Jake would—or could—give.

The Logan boys weren't the marrying kind.

But Mary…

No. He would not get emotionally involved.

Who was he kidding? He already was.

Which meant he had to help her, he thought as the long day wore on, as the deal finally reached its drawn-out conclusion, which meant the financial markets could relax for another week.

He thought of what the lawyer back in New Zealand had told him. 'She really is alone.'

If she was alone and in trouble…with his baby… There had to be a solution.

Finally at nine o'clock he signed the last document, left it on his secretary's desk and prepared to leave. But first one phone call.

Mathew Arden. Literary agent for some of the biggest names in the world.

'Well,' he said, as Mathew answered the phone. 'Am I right?'

She walked her legs off. She strolled down Fifth Avenue, she checked out Tiffany & Co., was awed by the jewellery and chuckled as the salespeople were lovely to her, even though they must know she could hardly afford to look at their wares.

She took the subway to Soho, just so she could say she'd been there, and spent time in its jumble of eclectic shops. She bought a pair of porcelain parrots for her next-door neighbour who was looking after Heinz.

She bought a truly awesome diamanté collar for Heinz. He'd show up every dog in the North Island.

She took the Staten Island ferry and checked out the Statue of Liberty from close quarters.

'You're just as beautiful as the pictures,' she told her lady-ship, and felt immeasurably pleased.

She ended up on Broadway and got a cheap ticket to see the last half of a musical she'd only ever seen on film.

She bought herself a hamburger, headed back on the sub-way to Ben's apartment—and was weirdly disappointed when he wasn't home.

She'd sort of wanted him to be impressed that she hadn't hung around all day waiting for him, but maybe she'd done too much trying to prove it. Her feet hurt.

She ran a bath and soaked, all the time waiting for his key in the lock.

'Just like I'm the little woman,' she told herself. 'Waiting for my man to come home.'

She let herself imagine it, just for a moment. If she and Ben were to take this further…

This'd be her life.

'Um, no,' she said, reaching out for a gorgeous-looking bottle of bath salts. Sprinkling it in. Lying back to soak some more. 'You know you never want to commit to some guy who'll turn out to be just like Dad. This is fantasy and nothing more.'

It was after ten when Ben reached home and he was feeling guilty.

This was what it'd be like if he ever tried marriage, he told himself. This was why Jake's marriage had foundered. The Logan boys' lives didn't centre round women. But still, the thoughts of the night before were with him. The memory of Mary in his bed was enough to make him turn the key with eagerness.

'Mary?'

No answer.

Her purse was on the counter. Her jacket was hanging on the chair. It felt good to see them. He liked it that Mary was in his apartment.

He checked his bedroom, half-hopeful that she'd be lying there as she'd lain last night.

'In your dreams,' he muttered. 'To have a woman wait for you...'

He checked her bedroom. She was curled in the centre of her bed, cocooned in pillows. She looked exhausted. She looked small and vulnerable and alone.

She looked...like Mary.

This woman was planning on returning to New Zealand to bear his child. With no support.

He didn't wake her. He headed to his study to think, and think he did. The idea that had been idling in the back of his mind all day was starting to coalesce into a plan.

It made sense—and Mary was a sensible woman.

He wasn't entirely sure how Heinz would fit in with the pedigree pooches who strutted round Central Park but he was pretty sure Heinz could hold his own.

Could Mary hold her own?

He was sure she could. In her own way she was as independent as he was.

He flicked open his laptop. There was work to be done, though not business. The financial world could manage without him tonight. Tonight Ben Logan was plotting a future for his child.

And his woman?

Be sensible, he told himself. There are levels of responsibility. You can take the practical route; just don't let the emotional side interfere.

CHAPTER ELEVEN

SHE WOKE AND FELT…lonely. This was crazy. How many mornings had she woken by herself in her life? Practically all of them, so what was different?

For a start, she was in Ben's apartment.

Yes, and tomorrow she was going home. Leaving.

Ben had inferred he wanted some input into their child's life. Did that mean he might visit? Or did it mean he might send for Ermintrude or whoever to visit him?

Worry about it when the time comes, she told herself.

He could have come to her when he got home last night.

He'd have been being kind. Letting her sleep.

'A pox on kindness,' she muttered.

She emerged and Ben was drinking coffee at the dining table. He had newspapers spread out before him but he wasn't reading. He was staring out over the park.

He turned and smiled and her heart did this crazy back flip with pike that she should be getting used to now. She wasn't.

'I didn't hear you come home. You should have woken me.' She sounded cross, she thought, and she tried to reel it in. She needed to be practical. She didn't need to admit that she wanted this man.

'You looked exhausted.'

She flushed, knowing she didn't look fantastic now either. Maybe she should have brought some hot lingerie for this trip. Maybe she should have at least brushed her hair before she'd emerged.

'You look great,' he said, and she thought again, *This man had some sort of telepathy going.*

'Says the man who didn't come to my bed last night. You could have, you know. You're hardly likely to get me pregnant.'

'Would you have wanted me to?'

And there was only one answer to that. Honesty. 'Yes,' she said. She managed a smile. 'Not…not that that's a come-on.'

'It's not taken as such,' he said, which flattened her because if he picked her up and carried her into his bedroom right now, she wouldn't object at all.

But he had no such intention. He looked…businesslike, she thought. He was wearing jeans and an open-necked shirt with the sleeves rolled up but he still managed to look sleek and clever. A man in control of his world.

A man not to be distracted by a woman in jogging pants.

'I promised you today,' he said. 'Coffee?'

'No, thanks, I've gone off it. A gallon of juice would be good. You don't need to do anything for me today.'

'What did you do yesterday?'

'Saw New York.'

'What, all of it?'

'As much as I could fit in. Statue of Liberty, Tiffany's, Fifth Avenue, Soho, Broadway, pastrami and rye sandwiches, bagels, New York cops being nice, wind coming up from under the pavements, markets, people, stuff.'

'Wow,' he said faintly. 'No wonder you slept.'

'My feet went to sleep first. Your pavements are hard.'

'Poor feet. So you don't want to walk today?'

'I might. With only one day left I won't waste it. But, Ben, you don't need to share.'

'I'm sharing,' he said brusquely. 'Four days to see America is ridiculous.'

'New York is enough.'

'It's not. What would you like to do?'

Go back to bed, she thought. *With you.*

She couldn't say it.

'I thought I might sit on a ferry,' she said. 'Just sit. I could see a heap and not walk at all.'

'So we're ruling out anywhere with pavements.'

'It's fine. Ben, you don't need to play travel escort.'

'No more city stuff?' he said, ignoring her.

'Ben…'

'Would you like to see my favourite place?' he asked. 'Somewhere I go to chill. When I have a business deal I need to clear my head from? Where I go to turn off?'

'That sounds like a bar.'

'It's not a bar,' he told her. 'Have you heard of the Adirondacks?'

'I… Yes,' she said. 'I mean…I guess I know it's a park of some kind.'

'A park,' he said, and snorted. He glanced out the window. 'Central Park's a park. I'll show you a park!'

'Isn't it…miles away?'

'You won't have to walk an inch, I promise. It's an amazing spring day, one out of the box. Let's take advantage of it. Okay, Mary Hammond, drink some juice and eat some toast while I do some phoning. Adirondacks, here we come.'

And two hours later, courtesy of a helicopter whose pilot greeted Ben like an old friend, Mary saw the Adirondacks.

First they flew over them.

'How can there be such a place so close to New York?' she breathed, looking down at what seemed endless mountains, rivers, lakes.

'It's our best-kept secret,' Ben told her through the headphones. 'It's bigger than almost all the country's national parks combined, enshrined in the constitution as a wilderness.'

At their landing place there were kayaks and a couple of burly men to help launch their craft. One kayak. One set of paddles.

'Because you're not paddling today,' Ben told her. 'This is your day of rest.'

'I can kayak.'

'It's pretty much floating. Give it a rest, Mary. Let me take charge.'

By which time she was flabbergasted. This was so far out of her league she was speechless.

'Just shut up and enjoy it,' he told her, so she did. This was another world. Ben's world. She wore one of Ben's big, warm jackets that smelled of him. She sat in the front of the kayak while Ben paddled behind and there was nothing to do but soak it in.

Ben paddled with the ease of a man who'd done this all his life. That made her feel…like she didn't know how to feel.

He took her along the Sacandaga River, into wilderness. There seemed to be no soul for miles, except for loons and ducks, and deer standing still and watchful on the river bank. When she saw a great bald eagle soaring in the thermals, even Ben seemed stunned.

'The eagles disappeared from here by the early sixties, but there's work to reintroduce them,' he told her. 'At last count we had twelve nesting pairs. It's a privilege to see them.'

She heard his awe and knew that for Ben this was indeed special.

'How often do you come here?'

'Often. Whenever I need to be alone.

You're almost always alone, she thought. *Surrounded by people, you're still alone.*

But she said nothing. This was not her business.

'I'm betting you help fund these wildlife projects,' she guessed.

'The company does fund wildlife projects,' he admitted, but he sounded brusque and she wondered why. Surely it wouldn't hurt to admit to being passionate about something.

But the more they paddled in this amazing place, the more the feeling of him as a loner intensified. What he'd told her of his family left her cold. Poor little rich boy.

He was a man in control. He was a financier, a commando, a billionaire.

Whatever, he seemed more alone than she was.

He paddled for miles, with strong, sweeping strokes that sped them along the calm surface of lakes and the streams that joined them. He must know where he was going. All she could do was trust him. All she could do was sit back and soak in the majestic mountains rising on either side of the banks, and the utter stillness, broken only by bird calls, the honking of geese and the weird calls of the stunningly marked loons.

The smell of the pine filled her senses. The sun was on her face and Ben was paddling with ease.

He did this often. Always alone? She guessed yes, and wondered if this was his only escape from the financial pressure he lived under.

Why did she keep coming back to his loneliness? Wasn't she the single mum? She should be worried about herself but, instead, the more she knew of this man the more her heart twisted for the isolation she sensed inside him.

She thought suddenly she'd vowed never to depend on a man. What if a man could be persuaded to depend on her?

It was a crazy thought but it shifted something inside. Something was changing. The defences she'd built up over so many years seemed to be cracking and she wasn't sure how to seal them again.

Ben was just…Ben. The man she'd held in her arms. A man she could hold in her heart?

It was a crazy thought, unthinkable, but against all reason the thought was there. What if…?

But the what-if stayed unspoken. Indeed, there seemed little need to speak at all. It was as if the wilderness itself was ordering them to be still.

Stop overthinking this, she told herself. Ben's a loner and he always will be. He's chosen his own course. Stop thinking and soak this in, because reality started tomorrow.

Alone for both of them.

* * *

This was make-believe. Time out.

Jake would approve, he thought. He was drifting through the most beautiful scenery in the world, with a beautiful woman…

Yep, it was playing make-believe, only it wasn't. She was a restful woman, his Mary. He could tell already that she loved this place. When he came here he could bring her…

Yeah, well, that was fantasy as well. His? She was a loner like himself. She wouldn't be his and he wouldn't be hers.

But they drifted on and the farther they went the more his plans came together.

This could work. He just needed Mary to think about it dispassionately, without emotion. There were two types of responsibility, he thought. One was tangible, the responsibility for keeping someone secure and protected. He could do that.

The other responsibility was emotional. His mother had demanded her children make her happy. He'd never ask that of anyone, neither would he expect the demand himself. Emotion needed to be set aside.

The problem was that for some reason, right now, emotion was everywhere.

The sun was on their faces. There was a rug stowed with a picnic hamper in the stowage area of the kayak. They could pull into shore, find a bed of pine needles and…

And not.

Today he had to be dispassionate. Today he needed to map out a sensible future for both of them.

Including a baby?

For all of them.

They ate lunch on the banks of the river, and the magnificence of the surroundings took her breath away.

Not enough, however, for her not to notice the lunch the guys at the landing place had handed them as they'd launched the kayak. Everything was in elegant, boxed containers, carefully labelled. Tiny bread rolls. Curls of golden butter. Crayfish, broken into bite-sized pieces. Tiny tomatoes, slivers of lettuce, radish, carrot, celery and a mouthwatering mayonnaise. Quiche in a container that had kept it warm.

éclairs filled with chocolate and creamy custard. Strawberries, watermelon, grapes.

Wine if she wanted, which she didn't. Two types of soda. Beer for Ben.

It should have been cold. They'd been drifting on fast-moving water from the spring thaw, but today…today it was summer.

Today was a day she'd remember for the rest of her life.

She ate the last éclair she could possibly fit in, stretched back on cushions—cushions!—and gazed up through the massive branches of a pine to the sun glinting through.

'This has been magic,' she whispered. 'Thank you so much for bringing me.'

'I could bring you once a month,' he said. 'Every time I come.'

It was said matter-of-factly, like a neighbour offering to share a shopping run. Once a month, take it or leave it.

'So you'd pop an airline ticket in the post for me once a month,' she managed when she got her breath back. This was fantasy. Maybe it was time they got out of here.

'I want you to stay.' He hesitated and then he said it. 'Mary, I want you to marry me.'

As a breathtaker it was right up there with the feeling she'd had when she'd looked at the blue line on her pregnancy-testing kit.

Maybe it was higher. She'd suspected she was pregnant. This had come from nowhere.

She'd been almost asleep, sated with the beauty of the morning, the food, the feeling of being with a man she felt instinctively would dive to her protection if a loon suddenly swooped to steal her éclair.

She wasn't asleep now.

I want you to marry me.

She glanced sharply at Ben, expecting to see him just as

dreamlike, making an idle joke that could be laughed off. Instead, she saw a man so tense there might be an army of loons lined up for attack.

'Wh-what?' She could barely get the word out. 'What do you mean?'

'I've spent twenty-four hours thinking about it,' he said. 'It's the only logical thing to do.'

She nodded, forcing herself to sound practical. Nurse humouring lunatic. 'Logical. I can see that.'

'Can you?'

'Um...no.'

'You won't be permitted to stay here unless we're married,' he told her. 'American immigration isn't welcoming to single mothers with no visible means of support.'

'Right.' She should sit up, she thought, but that'd mean taking his proposal seriously.

It didn't deserve it.

'I wasn't aware,' she said at last, 'that I wanted to live in America.' She glanced around and felt bound to add a rider. 'It's very nice,' she conceded. 'But it's not home.'

'Where's home?'

'In Taikohe, of course,' she said, astounded.

'Are you happy there?

'I have a job. I have neighbours. I have Heinz.'

'I've enquired about Heinz. We can get him over almost straight away.'

'To, what, live in your flash apartment?' This was the craziest conversation she'd ever had. 'Ben, what are you talking about?'

'I'm talking about us,' he said, and his voice said he wasn't crazy at all. His voice said this was a serious proposal. He'd put all the pieces of some weird jigsaw together and come up with a fully formulated plan. 'Mary, I've spent most of yesterday thinking this through. I would like to help you raise this child.'

Raise this child... That sounded mechanical, she thought. It sounded like following a recipe for making bread, or shifting a wreck off the ocean floor. *Raise this child...*

'How?' she managed, and apparently he really had thought about it.

'We're loners,' he told her. 'Both of us. We need our own space. That's a problem in that we need to raise this child together, but it's also good in that you have few ties to New Zealand. I've been trying to figure out how you could move to New York. I've run through the options, and the only one that'll work is marriage.'

'I…see,' she managed, but she didn't.

'You won't get a green card unless we do.'

'Why would I want a green card?'

'So you can stay here,' he said patiently. 'So I can have a say in raising this baby.'

'Will you stop saying "raising,"' she snapped, shock suddenly finding an expression. 'It's like building with Lego blocks. Producing something. A technical procedure. This is a baby we're talking about. A little person. You don't have to stand above and pull.'

'But it'll be work,' he said, refusing to be deflected. 'You can't want to bring it up by yourself.'

'I have Heinz—and my baby's not an *it*.'

'He—or she—will be my son or daughter, too.

'But you can't make me stay.' A niggle of fear suddenly grew much bigger. Had it been a mistake to tell him? He was a Logan. He had the world's resources behind him.

'I won't make you stay.' His voice gentled, as if he sensed her sudden terror and was backing off. 'How could I force you? But I want you to think about it. It could be good for both of us.'

'How would it be good?' she snapped. 'I know no one. I don't know if my nursing qualifications are acceptable. I have nowhere to live. I have nothing.'

'You could write,' he said, and shoved a hand into his pocket and produced a folded piece of paper. He handed it to her and then sat back and waited for her to read it.

She glared. She stared at the paper as if it contained explosives.

'Read it,' he said, gently, and she had no choice. And the letter took her breath away all over again.

Hey, Ben.
I'll admit I was pissed when you pushed me to read this so fast but now I'll admit to being impressed. This is raw talent and it's good. The story needs work but we could really take this places, especially if you're prepared to back us with publicity. It could be huge. Tell her to finish it and we'll go from there but if the end's as good as the beginning, we have a goer.

And then:

PS Her hero's sounding a lot like you, Ben, boy. Made me chuckle. She's good, your lady.

It was an email, dated late last night. From a publisher whose name was known throughout the world.

The words blurred into a black and white fuzz.

If the end's as good as the beginning, we have a goer.

She thought back to the cave, sitting writing what she loved. Using the time out. Writing Ben into her story.

He'd read it. He'd told her he'd read it.

Some time yesterday he must have copied it and given it to a publisher to read.

She should be thrilled, but…why did it feel such an invasion? Why did it feel he was almost taking over life?

'So here's my plan,' he said, before she could get her breath back. 'My apartment's huge. We won't need to stay this close long term but until you get your green card we need to live in the same premises to prove we're married. I'll get an architect in. We'll split the apartment so you have your quarters at one end, we'll put in a space for a nanny, and we can meet in the middle.

It'll need to be arranged so partitions can be set aside in case we have a visit from Immigration, but with a nanny, and me to take a role as well, you'll be free to write as much as you like.

'You can train Heinz to be an apartment dog—the park's just over the road. This could work.'

'You want me to live in your apartment.' She was having trouble speaking.

'You need help,' he said gently. 'I can't bear to think of you facing the future alone.'

'But marriage…'

'It's not exactly your standard proposal,' he said ruefully. 'We'll need a strong pre-nup agreement, but I'm trusting you.'

'Th-thank you?'

'I guess you'd be trusting me as well,' he said, smiling slightly. 'But I won't sue for half of Heinz.'

'You're thinking I'd sue?'

'It's not a real marriage but it'd work. It'd give you and the child security. It would mean I could keep in contact.'

'Why would you want to keep in contact?'

'Because this is my child.'

She was struggling to get her head around this. Struggling hard. He wanted to raise her child. He wanted to organise her writing. He wanted…what else?

'So you'd want to read bedtime stories and go to school plays? You'd want to change diapers and take sides when she faces school bullies?'

What was she gabbling about? she thought wildly. She was talking school plays? But the marriage thing was too big to consider. Marriage. Waking up beside this man, every day for the rest of her life.

But that wasn't what was on offer. What was on offer was assistance and control. This man didn't do close. Even the thought of the practicalities of child-rearing had him drawing back.

He'd really never thought of himself as a father? How lonely was he?

If the end's as good as the beginning…

The phrase from the publisher was suddenly front and centre.

She thought back to the cave, to holding each other, to mutual need. To the moment this baby had been conceived.

That had been the beginning. A joining of two people.

He was offering her an ending that was no such thing.

'The child-rearing would be over to you,' he said faintly. 'If you have a nanny, you should have time to cope with the odd diaper.'

'You don't want to share?'

'You keep your personal space and I'll keep mine.' He hesitated, then continued, but less sure, 'But, Mary, there is this attraction between us. Maybe we could keep that—if we both wanted.'

'With you living at one end of the apartment and me the other.'

'We could have visitation rights, to be decided as we go.'

He was joking?

He wasn't.

He'd plotted her future. She'd sit and write and care for their baby. Logan money would launch her book, which he'd organise to be published. *Her book*. Even her fantasy would be his. She'd be Mary Logan, author, promoted by the resources of the Logan empire. She'd live in New York and she'd have a nanny.

And she'd have a husband—*with visitation rights to be decided as we go*.

She was feeling just a little bit sick.

Actually, now she came to think about it, she felt a lot sick. Her body was taking over from her mind.

Ben must be able to see it. 'What's wrong?' he said sharply, but she waved him back.

'Just baby,' she said. 'Making its presence felt.' *It's telling me what it thinks of your stupid proposition,* she thought, but she didn't say it out loud. Her gorgeous day was spoiled.

He'd thrown her a sensible proposition to keep two loners staying as such. Why did it make her feel old and grey and ill? More and more ill.

'Leave me be for a moment,' she told him.

'Mary…'

'Leave me be.'

She had no choice. She could no longer face him.

She disappeared into the woods as fast as physical necessity dictated.

His first impulse was to follow. She was ill. She shouldn't be alone.

But, then, being alone was her right. Being alone was what his proposition was all about.

Except it wasn't. She'd be his wife. He'd be responsible for her—and for his child.

It freaked him out a bit, but he'd get used to the idea. He wouldn't get close enough to hurt them.

There was the rub. He'd been brought up in a household where sentimentality was exploited to ruthless effect. You protected yourself any way possible. You didn't get fond of nannies because they left—in fact, his father had come into his bedroom one night and found his nanny giving the twins a hug goodnight and the next day she was gone.

'I won't have any woman making my sons soft.'

There had been no softness in their house. His father had protected himself with his money and his power. His mother had manipulated him with emotion. She'd protected herself with her acting, and Jake had learned to do the same.

The one night his mother's acting had become reality, when he hadn't seen the difference, she'd died.

In time Ben had developed his own armour. He wasn't ruthless like his father. He didn't act. He simply held himself to himself.

The sight of Mary, shocked and ill, twisted something inside that hurt, but he knew that pushing to get closer wouldn't help. He'd help Mary practically but if she learned to rely on him emotionally he'd let her down.

He didn't know not to.

Raising a child… What had she said? You don't have to stand above and pull.

He didn't have a clue about child-raising. He only knew that he couldn't bear the thought of Mary going back to New Zealand.

Of Mary not having his resources available to her.

Of Mary being alone?

She was alone now.

She was ill. She wouldn't want him. She was a loner, just like he was.

So he forced himself to wait, packing the picnic gear, loading the kayak, making sure the site showed no traces of their stay. That's why he loved this place. He made no impression on it. It stood as it had stood for centuries, a place of solitude and peace.

It was a place where a man could be totally alone.

Except he wasn't alone now. Mary, was only yards away, being ill—because she was carrying his child.

Enough. The catering company who'd provided their lunch had provided napkins. He soaked a couple in the clear river water, and went to find her. He met her at the edge of the clearing. Whatever had happened was over. She looked wan and shaken and that same twist of his heart happened all over again.

He wanted to take her into his arms. He wanted to take her into his heart.

He didn't know how to.

For some reason he kept thinking of the night his nanny had been fired. Maggie was a loud, boisterous Australian. She'd bounced into their lives and she'd kept up with all the devilry he and Jake had thrown at her and more. For a while their lives had been fun.

Had he loved her? Maybe he'd started to, but one hug and she was gone.

He remembered his mother saying, 'Keep your emotions to yourselves, boys. I'm tired of interviewing nannies.' That was good, coming from his mother.

But if he fell for Mary…

Enough. He was putting neither of them at risk. Instead of hugging her, he proffered the napkins. Practical-R-Us.

'Thank you,' she said dully. 'And thank you for the proposal. It was well meant but I don't want it.'

'Why not?'

The question hung. She looked at him, just looked, and it was as if she was seeing everything he had to offer—and found it wanting.

'Because I'm not alone by choice,' she snapped. 'Because I love my community. I love my job and my roller-derby team and my dog. I love them. You don't get that, Ben, because you don't understand what love is, but I understand it. You're offering me a part of your world but that involves loneliness forever.'

She softened then, and the look she gave him was one of sympathy. Sympathy! No one offered Ben Logan sympathy but there it was.

'Ben, I know what love is,' she said, her voice bleak and flat. 'For a while I had my mum and my dad. I had my town and I had people who loved me. And it's precious. I know how precious is it, so I'll fight to get it back. Maybe I won't succeed but I'll try. Thank you for your offer. I understand how much it's taken to offer even so little of yourself but, Ben, I'm greedy. I want more and you aren't offering more. You can come and see us whenever you want. We'll work something out with our baby, but for now I want to go home.

Monday.

Her plane left at midday. She needed to be at the airport at ten. A cab might take an hour.

Therefore she stayed in her bedroom until nine. She hadn't slept all night but she was staying put. Ben knocked at seven, but she didn't answer. He'd knocked so lightly she could easily have been asleep—and how could she face him?

Marriage...staying here with Ben... In a way it was a siren call. She could stay here and hope. But hope was all she'd have, she thought. She'd be aching for him to want her. She'd be aching for him to be a part of her, and that wasn't what he was offering.

She'd be risking what had happened with her father. Loving a man and watching him turn away.

Nine o'clock. It was time to go. She needed to walk out without looking back.

Maybe Ben wouldn't even be here, she thought, not sure whether to hope or not. Maybe the knock on the door at seven had been to say goodbye.

Leaden hearted, she zipped her bag closed, gazed around the stupid cool grey room one last time, and walked out.

Ben was at the kitchen bench. A leather duffel was sitting by the door. A large duffel.

'H-hi,' she managed. Keep it simple, she told herself. Get it over with and ignore that bag. 'Could you call me a cab?'

'You need breakfast. You ate nothing last night and you lost your lunch.'

'I'll get something at the airport.'

'Eat here,' he growled.

'I don't have time.'

'Seeing the jet leaves when I say it leaves, you have all the time in the world.'

'R-right,' she managed. 'You'll ring the airline and say hold that plane?'

'I've organised our own jet.'

'You've…' She gasped. 'You've what?'

'Jake's in New Zealand, finishing up the movie he's working on. I'm therefore killing two birds with one stone. Seeing Jake. Taking you home.'

'In your dreams,' she said faintly.

He rose and headed to the other side of the bench. 'Toast?' he asked. 'One slice or two? No, make that two slices or three?'

She was hungry, she conceded. Morning sickness was a myth—it washed over her at any time it felt like it. Right now it was in abeyance and her stomach was telling her it was time to stock up.

But not at the expense of missing her plane.

'I'll have breakfast at the airport,' she told him, heading for the door. 'I'll hail my own cab.'

'So you'll sit in cattle class while I travel in luxury?'

'That's crazy. Flying your own jet all the way to New Zealand…just for one person.'

'Two if you come with me. That cuts our carbon footprint in half.'

'You have to be joking.'

'I'm not joking,' he said, and smiled at her, and, oh, that smile… She was wobbly anyway. That smile made her even more wobbly.

Maybe she needed to sit down.

'I'm…independent,' she managed.

'I know you are,' he agreed. 'That's one of the things I admire about you. But there's independent and there's pig stubborn. Come with me and you'll have your own bed, all the way to New Zealand.'

That caught her as nothing else could have. She still felt vaguely unwell. She'd flown over wedged between an overweight businessman and a harried mother who'd treated Mary as a free babysitter.

'My own…what?' she said cautiously.

'You heard. Full-size bed, with pillow menu.'

'You're kidding.'

He knew he had her. She could see it. His eyes got that twinkle she was starting to know, the one that said he was getting his own way. 'Pillows,' he said, like it was a siren call, and, oh, it was. 'I'd go for the double-size goosedown, with the neat Logan insignia on the pillowcase. Very classy.'

'It's a Logan plane?'

'Of course.' The toast popped. He flipped it onto a plate. 'Marmalade?'

She should get out of here. He'd clearly lost his mind.

Double-size goosedown…

'We provide pyjamas, too,' he added helpfully.

'It's not a double bed?' She was still trying to get her head around what he was offering, but her words came out as pure suspicion.

He grinned. 'You think I'd pay for a jet to fly to New Zealand just so I could get you back into bed?'

'I wouldn't put it past you.'

'The plane has full-size beds. One at either end of the plane.'

'How big's the plane?

'Big enough for you to jump me if you change your mind.' The twinkle grew.

'Ben...'

'I know.' His smile receded, but not far. 'You won't change, but, Mary, I can do so little. I respect your independence—of course I do—but allow me to make one last gesture. Let me take you home.'

And what was a girl to say? He stood there, smiling with that beguiling smile that would have caused harder hearts than hers to soften.

He didn't do the heart thing. She'd figured that. He was a man who kept himself apart and would continue to do so.

After he'd taken his private jet to New Zealand.

After she'd let him take her home.

CHAPTER TWELVE

HE THOUGHT SHE might talk to him during the flight. He thought he might even use the time to get her to change her mind.

Instead, she walked onto the plane, he showed her the bedroom set-up she could use and he lost her.

She looked at the piled pillows, the fluffy duvet, the magazines, the crystal glassware ready to be filled with anything she needed…

She yawned and smiled apologetically at Ben and the steward who accompanied them.

'Thank you so much,' she said. 'This is the stuff of dreams, and that's exactly where I'm going.'

So she slept, ensconced in privacy at her end of the plane. She didn't emerge.

Ben had also thought he might get some work done. He sat in front of his laptop and figures blurred.

He thought about independence and how much he valued it. He thought if he valued it, the least he could do was grant it to Mary.

He thought about Mary.

He'd arranged a car to be waiting at Auckland airport. Of course he had, Mary thought. It was a wonder it wasn't a limousine with chauffeur in attendance.

'I can catch a bus,' she said, but she was no longer in control.

'A four-hour bus journey? I don't think so. Why don't they have airports in Taikohe?'

'Because it's tiny. Ben, I'm fine. I'm nice and rested.'

'I'm not. Do you have a couch?'

'I…'

'I'll drive you home, stay overnight and head back tomorrow to see Jake.'

'You really do have it all planned.'

'I even have my international driving licence. Trust me?'

'No.'

'You want me to stay somewhere else?'

He'd paid for a jet to bring her all the way home. Maybe she could manage a sofa for the night. 'Fine.'

'Mary?

'Yes?'

'I'm not threatening your independence.'

'Believe it or not, that's not what this is about,' she told him. 'But it's okay, Ben. I accept your offer to drive me home and I won't threaten your independence either.'

To say Heinz was delighted to see her was an understatement. They arrived at her sparse little cottage and Mary had barely reached the front door before there was a hoy from the house next door and Heinz was tearing across the yard to meet her.

Mary fell to her knees, scooped him up and hugged him like she'd been away for months, letting him lick her. She even cried a little.

Over a dog?

But she meant it, Ben thought, remembering his mother's orchestrated emotion.

How did he know these tears were real?

He knew.

A middle-aged woman in farm-type overalls and mucky boots followed Heinz in. She enveloped Mary and dog in a bear hug and then turned to greet Ben. 'Hi,' she said, and stuck out her hand. 'I'm Mary's next-door neighbour, Kath. And you are?'

At least Mary had a neighbour, Ben thought. Mary's cottage was about a mile out of town but at least there was someone within calling distance. It should make him feel better, but it didn't.

'This is Ben, the guy I was stuck on the island with in the cyclone,' Mary said, emerging from Heinz's frenzied greeting. 'He's why I had to go overseas. I had to tell him I was pregnant.'

What followed was deep, uncompromising silence. Kath looked at him from the toes up, and then all the way down again.

'Pregnant,' she said at last.

'Yep.'

'Does your family know?'

'Not yet. You can spread it around if you want. They'll hear it in two minutes in this place.'

'You sure?'

'I'm sure I'm pregnant. The town might as well know.'

Ben was forgotten. Kath was staring at Mary, appalled. 'Mary, love, your stepmother and sisters will kill you. Sunrise's still blaming you for losing her baby. She'll say you've done it to spite her. You know your family. It's all about them. They'll have kittens.'

'I don't think it'll be that bad.'

'You know it will be.' But the woman checked Ben out again, and finally she began to smile. 'But you brought your guy home?'

'He brought me home.'

And the woman faced him square on. 'You staying? She'll need you.'

To say he was taken aback was an understatement. First, Mary hadn't told her next-door neighbour about her pregnancy before she'd left. Second, she was telling her now, and inviting her to share the news. She was telling the neighbourhood her business.

Why not? Did he want her to stay independent?

He wasn't sure what he wanted.

And, third, what the woman was saying was blunt and to the point.

She'll need you.

'He's not staying,' Mary said brusquely, pushing open the door. 'Or not more than a night. I don't need him. But thanks for caring for Heinz.'

'I have a casserole in the fridge. I'll bring it over.'

'I have stuff in the freezer. I'll be right on my own.'

'Mary, love…'

'Ben's staying tonight,' Mary told her. 'So I won't be eating baked beans by myself. And tomorrow I need to go back to work and get on with my life.'

He lay on her made-up-into-a-bed settee and stared into the night. The silence here was so deep it made him feel nervous. Somewhere outside a plover was making an occasional call to a distant mate, but there was nothing else. Nothing and nothing and nothing.

He was leaving her at the ends of the earth.

He thought the first time he'd seen her, on Hideaway Island, retreating even from this quiet place. She'd come back, though. She'd returned from her retreat and faced her world again. She was telling the world she was pregnant. She was facing them all down.

Her courage was breathtaking. He'd thought he was a loner but Mary had made it a life skill.

But still she needed…

Him?

Support, he thought. Someone to watch her back. Like him and Jake. For the last few years they'd gone their own ways, but they knew they were always there for each other.

Until now. He wasn't sure what Jake thought. The moments in the life raft had changed things.

They'd made him see how alone he really was.

But Mary needed him.

Three words kept blasting through his mind, refusing to let him sleep. She needs me.

How did she need him?

To face the community on her behalf? He suspected she had the courage to do that all by herself.

To whisk her off to New York and cosset her and keep her safe?

She wouldn't have it.

To just…be with her?

How could he do that? Where did he start? There was no common ground. He'd done all he could, asking her to stay in New York, yet she'd rejected it out of hand.

Maybe if he offered to knock a few walls down, share a bedroom…

Part of him wanted to. Part of him thought waking up next to this amazing woman for the rest of his life would be…

Terrifying. He'd hurt her.

Other people had successful marriages. He'd seen them; of course he had. Couples holding hands in public. Old men and women sitting peacefully at bus stations, their body language testament to a long life together.

He'd never trusted it.

Jake and his mother had learned to act to protect themselves, but he didn't have it—their ability to contain themselves while preserving an outer shell. That was why Jake had launched himself into his disastrous marriage while Ben knew he could do no such thing.

But he wanted Mary.

She was sleeping just through the door. The woman he wanted…

The fire was dying in the grate. Kath had set it so they'd just had to put a match to it as soon as they'd walked in. There was a small pile of chopped wood on the veranda and a mountain of logs out the back.

That was what he could do for her, he thought, and the idea gave him some peace. He'd spend another day here. He'd chop enough wood to last her through the winter.

Through her pregnancy?

He'd come back, he thought, when the baby arrived.

Before the baby came?

Okay, yes, because she couldn't have his baby alone.

She wanted to be alone.

There were too many thoughts playing in his head. He lay and watched the dying embers of the fire and thought about courage. He thought about one person's capacity to hurt another. He thought about independence.

'I'm better off getting out of her life now,' he told the darkness. 'I'll do what I can, but it has to be from a distance.'

The phone rang at five minutes past seven. Ben was already out on the veranda, checking out the wood situation.

Mary emerged in her nightie. She still looked pale, he thought. How long did morning sickness last? Had she been ill in the night?

'You're still here,' she said, and she sounded almost surprised.

'I'm staying for one more day,' he growled. 'I'll leave you with enough wood to keep you going through the pregnancy.'

'You don't need—'

'I do. Grant me that much, Mary.'

She looked at him for a long moment and then nodded. 'Thank you. But I need to go to work.'

'Already?'

'I'm on call, starting today. I took as much leave as I had, at Hideaway and then going to the States. I'm on call as of now and the phone's been switched through. Ross Scythe lives on the ridge with his wife, Ethel. Ross's had a fall but he's refusing to let Ethel call an ambulance. I need to go.'

He looked at her. She looked at her nightie.

She smiled but her smile was a bit wonky. She must still be feeling ill.

'I'll get dressed first,' she conceded.

'Very professional. And breakfast?'

'You're always pushing toast at me. I'll eat on the run. But, Ben, it means you'll be here by yourself.'

'I'm fine by myself.'

'Of course you are.' Her face changed, but before he could react she'd headed inside to get ready.

Only then her car wouldn't start. Flat battery.

'I use the district nursing car,' she said, frustrated. 'But I need to get down to the hospital to collect it.'

'We could use jump leads to start it. Do you have jump leads?'

'No,' she said crossly, and kicked a tyre in frustration. She looked cute, Ben thought. She was in her district nursing uniform, plain green pants and white blouse with nursing insignia on the breast. Her cropped curls were damp from her shower, framing her face beautifully.

If he lived in Taikohe he'd like a district nurse who looked like this, he thought. The way she looked, she was guaranteed to make a man feel better.

She was still pale.

'I'll drive you,' he said.

She looked worried, glancing at her watch. 'Thanks, but, Ben, timewise…I should get you to take me into town so I can get the work car, but Ross has been on the floor for half an hour already. His place is only a mile further out. Do you think you could drive me there first?'

So he drove her to see her patient. He sat in the car while she went inside. Then she called him.

'I think Ross has just twisted his knee,' she said. 'It might be broken but I doubt it, and he has someone coming to talk to him this morning about buying cows. Very important. I'll organise the ambulance to pick him up and take him down to the hospital for X-rays afterwards but meanwhile could you give me a hand to lift him off the floor?'

'You're not lifting anything,' he said, startled, and she gave him an exasperated stare.

'Ben, I know what I can and can't do and that's why I'm asking you for help now. It's one of the reasons I came to New York to tell you about the baby. I know when I need to share. Share or not, Ben Logan? Lift.'

So he helped Mary get the elderly farmer into a fireside chair and followed instructions while Mary got him dressed in respectable, farmer-type clothes.

'So I can greet this guy looking like I know how to cut a deal. If he thinks I'm a sook he'll lower his price,' Ross told them, while his wife looked worried.

'Heaven help anyone who thinks you're a sook,' Mary retorted. 'Take the painkillers and the ambulance will be here in three hours. If you're not in X-Ray by lunchtime I'll be out here to get you, even if it means both of us walking.'

'You're a hard woman,' Ross said, but he was smiling. He glanced at Ben. 'So you're her bloke?'

'Um...'

'Ben's the guy I pulled out of the water during the cyclone,' Mary said. 'He's the father of my baby.'

And there it was again, his business, out in the open for everyone to inspect.

She had no right...

Except she did have the right, he thought. She was pregnant. He was the father. Why not say it so the district wouldn't spend the next few months playing guessing games?

'Oh, my dear,' Ethel breathed. She fixed Ben with a look that pierced. 'So you'll marry her?'

'It doesn't work like that these days,' Mary said, packing her bag with brisk efficiency. 'They've banned shotguns.'

'I asked her,' Ben said, thinking if she was going to be honest, he could be, too. 'She's refused.'

'He looks okay to me,' Ethel said. 'What's wrong with him?'

'Ethel, why did you marry Ross?' Mary demanded, closing her bag with a loud snap.

'I can't remember.' And then Ethel gave a faint smile and turned her attention to a framed photo on the mantel of a young

Ethel and Ross on their wedding day. 'Okay, I thought he was lovely,' she conceded. 'I wanted to spend the rest of my life with him. No one told me how pig-headed he'd be. We went into our wedding in a cloud of soap bubbles.'

'Do you ever regret it?' Mary asked bluntly, and Ethel coloured. She looked down at Ross and coloured some more.

'I guess not,' she conceded at last. 'He's stubborn and he drives me nuts and dints are everywhere in the fairy-tale image, but enough of the soap bubbles remain.'

'Well, that's why I'm not marrying,' Mary told her. 'I know about the dints, I know about stubborn and I know about independent. My father turned his back on me and it broke my heart. Loving's a huge risk and I'm not being offered one single soap bubble to make up for it.'

'What did that mean?' Back in the car they were headed into town so she could get her car and start her day's work properly.

'What?'

'Soap bubbles.'

'Fantasy,' she said crisply. 'Little girl's dreams. Two hearts become one. Romantic fluff.'

'Is that what you want from me?'

'I don't want anything from you. I told you that. You've made me an offer and I've refused. I'm taking my dreams elsewhere.'

'So you'd like romantic fantasy from someone else?'

'If a hero appears on my horizon maybe I'm available, but he'd have to be something to be worth the risk.' She said it lightly but he sensed a faint note of longing behind the words. Had he imagined it? Did this fiercely independent woman long for romance with all the trappings?

If he had been Jake, he could have supplied it, he thought.

He wasn't play-acting. Life was real. Life was for holding yourself together so you didn't hurt anyone else.

He couldn't supply anything.

* * *

'Is it okay if I stay tonight?' he asked as he dropped her off at work.

'Fine by me,' she managed, although it wasn't. The sooner this man got out of her life, the sooner she might find some sort of equilibrium. Maybe.

'Jake's on location today. He won't be back until tomorrow so I've set the flight back a day.'

That caught her. 'You're seeing Jake only once before you leave? You've come halfway round the world to see him for less than a day?'

'That's like someone I know coming from half a world away to tell me something she might have told me on the phone.'

He was teasing, but she wasn't to be deflected. 'I thought you and Jake were close.'

'Not close.' His voice grew crisp. 'We were dependent on each other when we were kids. We were stupid together. Hopefully we're past that now.'

'Right.' Work was waiting. She knew there'd be a full list of patients. They'd had no one to replace her while she was away and the work would have banked up. She had to go.

But Ben was sitting right next to her.

It didn't matter, she told herself. He was a loner. He didn't need her company and she didn't need his.

But she didn't want to leave.

'I'll bring home fish and chips for dinner,' she told him.

'I'll do dinner.'

'There's no catering in Taikohe.'

'What an insult,' he said, and grinned. 'Go to work and leave the domestic stuff to me. I can manage.'

I bet you can, she thought as she headed inside. It nearly killed her not to turn and watch his car disappear. But managing—alone—that was what Ben Logan was all about.

Work engulfed her. It was after six before she finally finished. Doreen, Taikohe's medical administrator, dropped her off at the cottage with a cheery offer to pick her up the next day and give her a loan to cover the cost of a new car battery.

She accepted the first offer and refused the second. She had enough funds to cover a battery.

Weariness engulfed her as she climbed from the car and headed for the house, a wash of grey fatigue. She'd been feeling nauseous all day. Now, suddenly, she wanted to sit on the front step, put her head in her hands and sleep.

Because Ben was leaving tomorrow?

Because she was facing having Ben's baby alone?

The thought of a long pregnancy with no one beside her was suddenly overwhelming.

She wanted her mother.

She wanted…Ben?

'Because you're pregnant and your hormones are all over the place,' she told herself crossly. 'Get over it. Women have managed on their own for generations. You don't need a male, especially a money-oriented, risk-taking loner like Ben Logan.'

Heinz had come tearing around from the back of the house to greet her. The sound of wood-chopping was echoing over the yard. Ben.

For some reason she didn't want to face him.

Wimp. He'd be gone tomorrow. She could do this.

She rounded the corner of the house to find a mountain of chopped wood stacked against the shed. Ben had his back to her, and the sight made her forget about weariness, forget about nausea. He was wearing boots and jeans and nothing else.

A sheen of sweat covered his skin. The sun was low in the sky, glinting on his broad, muscled back. His hair was ruffled and his boots were grubby.

He had a tattoo. She hadn't noticed it before but a Chinese symbol was etched beneath his armpit.

She had an almost irresistible urge to walk forward and touch it. Somehow she didn't, but it was close.

He looked a world away from the self-contained financier

she knew he was. For just a moment she let herself imagine how it could be if he was here, always. A man to come home to.

Like 'the little wife.' A man, ready with his slippers and pipe.

She smiled but the smile was self-mocking.

But still she looked, soaking in the sound and sight of him. This would have to last her forever.

Finally, Heinz, obviously impatient that she wasn't joining him with his new best friend, rushed back to her and barked, and Ben turned and saw her.

He smiled, and with that smile she knew she was in real trouble. This man did things to her heart that she didn't know how to handle.

He was the father of her baby and she loved it that she'd have a part of him forever. But she wanted more.

So go back to New York with him. Accept his offer.

But that was the way of isolation, and she was sensible enough to know it. Romantic fantasy had to be weighed against reality.

Reality was here, now, where Ben was smiling at her.

'This'll keep me going for the millennium,' she managed, motioning to the wood. 'Thank you.'

'It's the least I could do. I've also bought you a new battery.'

'I… Thank you. How much—?'

'Don't be daft. Oh, and I got you a refund on your return fare. I had my secretary cancel your return booking before we left so you'll get a refund.'

Whoa…

'And I'll transfer a set amount to your bank account each month,' he said. He hadn't moved; he was standing amid chopped wood, naked from the waist up, holding his axe, discussing money like it was nothing. 'As the mother of my baby, outside work should be optional.'

'No!'

He didn't answer. One eyebrow hiked, as he stood and waited for her to explain.

As the mother of my baby, outside work should be optional…

What was there in that to make her cringe? What was there to make her back away?

'Work isn't optional,' she told him, and she knew as she said it that she was speaking the truth. Money or not. 'I need...to be needed.'

'Our baby will need you.'

'It's not enough.'

'Mary...'

'You don't get it,' she said. 'You can't. I know that. But thank you for your offer; it's wonderful and generous and I should say yes. But I can't. If you'll set up a trust fund so I can use it for our baby's expenses, education, that sort of thing, I'd appreciate it enormously.'

She summoned a grin, and heaven only knew the strength it took. 'I might even use it to buy a fancy pram. But you'll be paying for your child, Ben, not for me. You and I came together in a storm but that's all it was. A storm. A flash of blood to the head and that was it.'

'You know there's more to it than that.'

'I might know it,' she said. 'But that doesn't mean I intend being Ben Logan's kept woman, wife or not. Your money's between you and our child.' She paused and looked at his wood pile. It was...astonishing. 'But thank you for the wood.' She hesitated, searching for distraction. 'Um...what's the tattoo?'

'It's the symbol for twins,' he told her. 'Jake has one, too. Joined at the breastbone.'

'Are you, though?' She found the idea strangely troubling. This man was so alone. He was standing in the setting sun, facing her, solitary, tough and isolated. For some reason his isolation was doing something to her heart.

There was nothing she could do about it, though. But maybe Jake... 'How often do you see him?' she asked.

'Often enough,' he said, and there was that in his face that told her not to go there.

But she did. Of course she did.

'Ben, this tension between you? Can I help fix it?'

'It's nothing I can't handle.' He slammed his axe into the log he'd been chopping and she knew there was no way he'd share.

This man never shared. Not emotionally. She'd figured that about him now.

Ben Logan, solitary man.

Beautiful man.

'There's lasagne in the oven,' he told her, and she forced herself to stop looking at his body, stop worrying about the unknown Jake, stop feeling sorry for Ben who stood alone because he'd made that choice.

'Kath brought it over?'

'I made it myself!'

'You're kidding me.'

'You don't go straight from rookie to commando in the army,' he said, and somehow his smile reappeared. 'I was appalled to learn there were halfway steps. I was assigned six months' mess duty when I first enlisted. I can now feed battalions.'

'So how much lasagne are we talking?' she asked cautiously, and he grinned.

'Maybe not enough to feed a battalion but I have filled the freezer. I do a mean chicken pie, too. I've made you six.'

'Wow.' She was trying desperately to sound flippant. Inside she was choking. 'Thank…thank you. You want to come and eat? I seem to have enough wood for a battalion as well.'

'I'll pay for someone to chop more when you run out.'

'There's no need—'

'Keeping my baby warm is my need.'

She swallowed. He'd be part of her life from now on, she thought. Part and yet not part. There'd be money arriving when she most needed it, money and help.

But not Ben.

She turned back to the house, unable to look at him. He was doing her head in with the way he looked. He was one gorgeous guy. He was vulnerable and isolated and he wasn't letting anyone in.

'Is there anything wrong?' he asked, as she headed indoors?

'Nope,' she flung over her shoulder. 'What could possibly be wrong?'

They ate dinner in near silence.

'How was your day?' he asked, and she managed a smile.

'The line is, *How was your day, dear?*'

He smiled back, but he didn't feel like smiling. He was all at sea, he admitted. He'd worked himself into the ground all day, trying to do as much as possible for her before he left. Now, with nothing left to do but sit across the dinner table from her, he felt lost.

In the morning he'd walk away. She needed nothing else from him.

If only she'd eat a bit more…

'If I eat more I'll throw up,' she told him. 'Little, often, that's how I'm handling it. I'll snack at midnight.'

He wanted to be around to make sure she did.

She had Kath next door.

One neighbour wasn't enough.

'I'll phone you often to make sure…'

'I don't need phone calls,' she said gently. 'Ben, your relationship will be with our baby, not with me.'

'I'd hope we can be friends.'

'Can you be friends with a guy you've slept with? I'm not sure.'

'We can try.'

'Okay,' she said, but sounded doubtful.

'So phone calls?'

'If you must.'

'Mary…'

'That's it, then,' she said, rising and clearing dishes with noisy efficiency. 'Great lasagne. Thanks, Ben.'

And then the phone rang and she grabbed it as if it was a lifeline. She listened for a moment and then nodded.

'Okay. See you in fifteen.' She disconnected and smiled apologetically. 'Sorry, Ben, I need to go out.'

'Roller derby?'

'How did you guess? They're a man short and it's a final. They were hoping I'd be back.'

'Should you—?'

'First trimester should be okay. Baby's tiny and nicely buffered and the Taimarana Terrors are skilled rather than rough. We play them often. Will you be right here by yourself?'

'Of course I'll be right,' he said, and he couldn't hide an edge of anger behind his words. 'But I'd like to come with you.'

'How are you at counting?'

'What?'

'We're always short on referees. Timer, or maybe a jammer referee if you think you're up to it. How do you feel about wearing a helmet? It's to identify which team you're watching.'

'I know that.'

'You do?'

'I read up on it. How could I not research the interests of the mother of my child?'

'I see.' She sounded disconcerted but she was in a rush. The dishes were forgotten—she was flying around, collecting gear.

'Mary?'

'Mmm?'

'You're pregnant.'

'So I am.'

'It's a contact sport. I don't think you should be playing.'

She paused and looked at him. She glanced down at her tummy and suddenly he saw a wash of something that looked like grief cross her face.

'I... Soon.'

'What do you mean, soon?'

'I'll give it up when I need to.'

'Mary—'

'Not yet,' she said, almost fiercely. 'For the first trimester there's so much amniotic fluid compared to baby size that I'd need to be hit by a truck to make a difference.'

'From what I see, isn't that what roller derby is? Trucks all over the place.'

'The team we're playing tonight is more tactical.'

'But not all teams?'

'Not all,' she admitted. 'So I do need to give it up.' She glanced down at her tummy and once again there was a wash of grief. 'But not yet,' she whispered almost fiercely. 'Not unless I have to. I'll hold to what I have for as long as I'm able.'

She was amazing! Smash 'em Mary was stunning.

The team greeted her with joy; 'We've missed you and, wow, we need you!' She stuck on a helmet bearing two stripes.

The stars meant she was designated jammer.

He could see why. This woman was good.

He'd figured out the rules by now. Mary's job was to pass the entire pack of the opposite team; all the women designated as blockers. Once she got past everyone, the team's score depended on her. She won points for every additional blocker she passed after she'd lapped the entire team.

She was little and quick and agile. She darted in and out of the pack, past women twice her size. The blockers skated to cut her off, using their bodies to keep her behind them, but Mary wouldn't be kept. She weaved with a skill that kept him breathless. She was flying, and she was loving it. From the sidelines the Tigers' supporters whooped her on. Ben was supposed to be keeping time—he was!—but he was whooping, too.

But, hell, some of these women were big. Mary fell once and it was all he could do not to dive out onto the track and grab her. But she was on her feet again, laughing, and flying past the girl who'd just tripped her up.

The more he saw, the more astounded he became. He'd read about this game. He'd watched it on YouTube, but what he hadn't appreciated on the screen was the need for teamwork. You could sit on the sidelines and see a mass of women flying round the track, but when you watched just the one woman you saw how protected she was, and how protective. Each woman was looking out for her teammates. The team was a unit, cohesive and powerful in a way that took his breath away.

The Taikohe Tigers won by a lot and it didn't take the way the women crowded around Mary at the end to know much of that win was down to her. Her team was brilliant but Mary—*his Mary*—was one out of the box.

He felt like shouting it. *My Mary rocks.*

But… But…

She's not my Mary, he told himself savagely. He was leaving tomorrow. He was heading back to Manhattan. Alone.

Leaving Mary with her tribe?

She'd pulled off her skates and helmet, tugged on her coat and was heading towards him. It felt…good, he thought, that this amazing woman was walking towards him.

There was a dumb thought. He'd driven her here. Of course she had to come with him.

'What did you think?' She was lit up like a Christmas tree, exhaustion and happiness radiating in equal measure. 'Wasn't that awesome?'

'Awesome.' There were some things a man just had to agree with.

'I won't be able to do it much longer,' she said, and once again he saw that trace of grief. 'I'll miss it so much. These women are my pack.'

And he'd seen it. The way they'd greeted her, the skill of the blockers as they'd protected her, the yelling of the pivot—the head blocker—aimed at keeping her safe, giving her passage, but more, the underlying respect each woman had for each of the others.

He'd seen this type of respect in the army, in a tight-knit battle situation where every soldier depended on the others for their life.

He'd struggled with it in his personal life, the closeness of interconnecting need. He'd decided he could do without it.

But Mary was loving it. He could see it as she looked back at her team and he could see the regret.

'I'll miss them so much...'

'Hey!'

She turned and there was a woman coming through the door towards them. A woman with vitriol written all over her face.

She was middle-aged, wearing too much make-up, clothes that were frankly tarty. Peroxide blonde. Buxom. Looking rigid with anger. She walked straight up to Mary, and before he could react, before anyone could react, she slapped her hard across the cheek.

Mary's face snapped back and then Ben was between them, grabbing the woman's arm as she raised her hand again, forcing it down.

'What the hell do you think you're doing?'

'And who are you?' The woman's voice was shrill with hate. 'The guy stuck on that island? The stud that got her pregnant? They say you're rich.' She turned back to Mary. 'Is that why you did it, you slut, or did you do it just to hurt Sunrise?'

'I didn't!' Mary sounded appalled, justifiably. She was wearing a handprint inflamed across her cheek. 'I didn't mean—'

'You killed your sister's baby. You think you might have one yourself now, just to rub it in?'

'Leave it, Barbie.' The woman who'd played pivot, still on her skates, headed across to intervene. 'You know everyone says it wasn't Mary's fault. That lawyer who was here—'

'I know what I know,' Barbie hissed. 'And I know that this woman is a slut. I told you before, keep her out of your team. I can't stop her working, but I can tell anyone who socialises with her, forget about coming to our pub. Forget about anyone connected to you getting anywhere in this town. You know my husband's money controls this place. We might have to put up with her but we don't have to like her.'

'Barbie—'

'And you, Hayley Durant,' the woman snarled, poking a painted fingernail into the pivot's chest. 'Your husband works for Small's Hardware. My husband owns the freehold on that store. You keep playing nice with *her* and he'll be shown the door.'

'If that happens,' Ben said, starting to figure who this woman must be and what power she had, 'then I'll move in. You've already had a hint of what my lawyers can do. Believe me, that's just a taste. I have money and I have power, and I'll use whatever it takes to keep Mary safe.'

'You can keep her safe,' Barbie snarled. 'But you can't keep her accepted. She's an outsider here. She doesn't belong.'

'But I don't need to belong,' Mary whispered. 'No, it's all right, Hayley. Barbie's right, I'm pregnant so I need to give up roller derby anyway. As long as I can keep working…and she can't stop me doing that…'

'Where's your father in all this?' Ben demanded. 'Why isn't he standing up to this woman?'

'Because he's not strong enough,' Mary whispered. 'Because he loves Barbie and his stepdaughters. He stopped loving me a long time ago.'

'And you?'

'I don't need him,' she told him. 'You have it right. We don't really need anyone. You can do it, so I can do it. No, it's okay, Hayley, no one needs risk anything on my behalf. It's okay, Ben, I don't need you to defend me. I'm fine on my own.'

'I'll take you home.'

She glanced at her watch. Nine o'clock. 'There's still time,' she said.

'Time for what?'

'You're going back to your isolation,' she said. 'The Adirondacks are your refuge? Let me show you mine.'

She was tired to death. She should just let him take her home but she couldn't bear it.

She wanted him so much…so seduce him with her country? It was a crazy thought, but she was past thinking whether things were crazy or not. All she could think of was that she had this one last night.

This one last chance.

She directed him to the coast, ten minutes' drive away. They pulled up at a collection of motley fishing sheds and a rickety jetty, all dark and deserted They overlooked an inlet, surrounded by mountains on three sides, deep and mysterious, almost a landlocked bay where he couldn't see the outlet to the sea.

'This used to be the base of a fishing community,' she told him. 'But the entrance has silted up. The inlet's still tidal but the water's so shallow at the entrance boats can't get in and out. So it's pretty much a private place.'

The night was completely still. The moon hung low over the water, a shimmery haze. Magic.

'You want to row?' she asked.

'You're kidding.'

'I can row but I'm tired.'

'There's a boat?'

'One of my old patients keeps a rowboat in the far shed and lets me use it. I have a key.'

'Why—?'

'Because I want to show you that I have everything you have and more,' she told him. 'You have a fancy apartment and a housekeeper. I have a cottage and a dog. You have enough money to keep you satisfied and so do I. I have a community as well. This is my final trump card. Adirondacks, eat your heart out.'

It didn't make sense but he was past trying to make sense of what was happening. He was out of his depth and he knew it.

She led him to the last boat shed, inserted a rusty key and found the boat.

The rowing boat was surprisingly neat. The doors of the shed were still oiled. They swung open to the inlet and they were away.

And the moment the boat shed was behind them, he knew why she'd brought him here. He'd visited New Zealand for forty-eight hours but he'd seen nothing. It no longer mattered. For the rest of his life, whenever he thought of this country he'd think of this place.

The mountains loomed majestically around them. The night was whisper quiet. The moon was a vast ball, hung so low and near it was as if they could reach out and touch it.

Flocks of wild swans drifted lazily on the water's surface. As they neared each group, the birds rose, the sweep of their wings on the darkened water a sound he'd remember forever.

Why had she brought him here? It didn't matter. He was awed, as she'd obviously expected him to be awed. She sat quietly in the bow of the boat and he thought…he'd never known such a woman.

And he thought, *She had to marry him.*

'This place is magic,' he said at last into the stillness. 'You're right, it has everything. But for you… You can't tell me you row here at night alone?'

'I do.'

'It's not safe.'

'No,' she said sadly. 'I won't do it again. Not now I have my baby to think of.'

'Our baby.'

'Yes,' she said, and fell silent.

'Everything's changing,' he said softly. 'There's so much, and you're so alone everywhere.'

'I have my job and my workmates. I have Kath next door. The girls in my team will be here for me in emergencies.'

'It'd take a real emergency for them to defy Barbie.'

'Barbie's fury will blow itself out. Things will settle. And my baby will have a community.'

'Is that what this is all about? Hope for a community?'

'Maybe it is.'

'Is it about your dad?' he guessed. 'Are you still hoping?'

She thought about it, while she gazed out at the silhouettes of the swans drifting against the moonlight.

'Maybe I am.' Then she raised her chin and met his gaze, defiant. 'I still love him.'

'Mary, he's never there for you.'

'Once upon a time he was,' she said sadly. 'There was my mum and my dad and me. And then when Mum died there was just Dad and me. Barbie killed that. Dad was wiped by Mum's death and Barbie picked up the pieces, but he's never been whole again. She controls him, but underneath somewhere Dad's there.'

'You'd stick around to wait for him to find the courage to break free? You'd give up everything for something that might never happen?'

'Tell me, Ben,' she said, and she was suddenly sure of herself again, 'what would I be giving up?'

'I can give you a life.'

The chin stayed tilted. 'You can give me an apartment. A place to write. Money for child-raising. As your wife I'd probably have money for stuff I haven't thought of yet. But you wouldn't be giving me yourself.'

'I don't know what you mean.'

'I think you do, Ben,' she said gently. 'You saw it today, with Ross and Ethel. Soap bubbles. That's what they have and they've lived with them for all their lives. I know they may burst at any minute but my mum and dad had them in spades.' She took a deep breath and seemed to firm.

'I know it may never happen for me,' she said softly. 'Especially now I seem—stupidly—to have given my heart to a man called Ben Logan. Ben, I've used my writing as a fantasy and, yes, as a shield. The thought of loving someone, leaving myself open to the sort of pain I felt when Dad turned away from me, has always left me terrified.

'But with you...I have no idea why, but for some stupid reason I'd risk it all. If I let myself love you I could abandon that fantasy. But living down the hall from you and still needing that escape—it'd break my heart. That's not a guess, it's a certainty, and I can't do it.'

'Mary—'

'No.' He'd reached out for her but she held out her hands to ward him off. The boat wobbled and he couldn't move.

'I shouldn't have said that,' she managed. 'More. I shouldn't have made love to you. I shouldn't have got pregnant. Maybe I shouldn't even have told you I was pregnant, but, then, dishonesty's not my way. Okay, I've fallen in love with you and maybe I did the first time I saw you. I have no idea why, or when, or what to do with it, but somehow it'd happened. I don't know how to stop it, but loving you without reciprocation would kill me. Maybe that's me being dumb. Maybe that's why I stay here, hoping against hope my dad will love me again.

'The closest I've ever had to belonging is with my team, my Tigers. Ben, I loved playing again tonight, the closeness, the mutual dependence, the power of more than one. I love sitting here now while you row me, but I need to let it go. I need to let you go. Yes, I'm on my own—but I'm not heading to Manhattan because that way I'll be alone forever.'

And he didn't know how to reply.

She loved him. He wanted to take her into his arms, but rowboats weren't built for passion. And her body language said he shouldn't even try.

'You'll have your baby,' he managed. 'In Manhattan...you won't be alone.'

'*My* baby? That's just it, isn't it, Ben? Sometimes you say it's yours. Sometimes you say ours, but you still feel like it's mine. That's okay. The baby and I will be a unit, but where will you be?'

'If you're in Manhattan I'll be there when you need me.'

'How will you know when I need you? There won't be a pile of unstacked wood. The nanny will do the hard bits. How can you possibly know when I need you?'

'You'll be safe.'

'I'm safe here, Ben. Barbie's not going to eat me.'

He reached out then and took her hand. He tugged her slightly towards him and for some reason she didn't resist. The boat rocked again but he was careful. Very careful.

He touched her cheek. He could feel the heat from the imprint of Barbie's hand. That he hadn't been fast enough to stop her almost killed him.

'It's okay, Ben,' Mary said softly. 'She's the worst of my dragons and, as far as you can, you've slayed her for me. You've done all you can. You can go back to the States with a clear conscience.'

'I can't let you go.' He hadn't meant to say it. It had just come out. He tugged her closer and he felt her yield.

He held her; he just held her, and she let herself be held. For a long, long moment they stayed close while the boat rocked gently in the moonlight. He could feel her breathing against him. His face was in her hair.

He was holding his woman.

She loved him. Maybe if he said it back...

But he didn't know how to. The words were there but they wouldn't come out.

'I'm sorry,' he said at last into her hair, and he felt things change. She'd been leaning into him, seemingly taking warmth and strength from his body. Now she gathered herself and pulled away.

'I'm sorry, too, Ben,' she whispered. 'But thank you for trying. If you ever figure it out... If you ever figure out what love is... Well, I've waited for my dad for twenty years. A few more years won't hurt.'

'And if someone else comes?'

'I hope he does,' she said with sudden asperity. 'If any hero happens by on his white charger, with his heart nicely on his sleeve where I can catch it and hold it, then I won't look back. But that's none of your business, Ben Logan. How long I wait and how much I break my heart while waiting is entirely up to me.'

* * *

They drove home in silence. She ate dry toast and went to bed with hardly a word.

He woke in the night to hear her being ill, and he felt...well, bad was too small a word to describe it.

Why not walk in there, take her into his arms and tell her he loved her? For he did love her, he knew it. The thought of walking away was almost killing him.

But other thoughts kept superimposing themselves, almost as if mocking. The sight of his brother, bloodied and unconscious on a dirty road in Afghanistan. His mother coming home late at night from the theatre, high on adrenalin and who knew what else, hugging him, saying, 'Keep me happy, Ben, make me stay happy.'

Looking in his mother's bedroom doorway the morning she'd died and seeing how he'd failed.

Half a dozen steps would take him to Mary's door and he couldn't take them. If he was to let her down...

Surely leaving her here was letting her down, but taking her back...on her terms...

Her manuscript was lying on the kitchen table. He flicked through it, half smiling but close to tears. In fiction anything could happen. In fiction he could even be a hero.

In her imaginary world, Mary could be safe. What sort of world could he give her where she'd be safer?

This was doing his head in. He rose, half hoping to see Mary coming out of the bathroom, but she was back in the bedroom with her door closed tight. She and Heinz and baby, a team. She'd let him in if he asked, he thought, but it was all or nothing. And all was more than he could give.

Instead, he walked outside and gazed up at the stars, at the Southern Cross hanging low in the night sky. He didn't belong here, he told himself. He had to leave.

He had to walk away from Mary.

'There's nothing else I can do,' he told himself. 'Happy ever after…she can have that in her writing. There's no way I can give it to her. I'd risk breaking all of us.'

Dawn. Time to leave. Jake had post-production meetings all day and wouldn't be able to see him until evening, but staying was doing his head in. He needed to get back to Manhattan, to an unemotional world, where things made sense.

He knocked on Mary's bedroom door, feeling ill himself.

'Come in.'

She was still in bed, looking wan and pale and incredibly small, huddled under her bedclothes.

'How sick—?'

'I'm fine,' she said, managing a rueful smile. 'Okay, I'm not fine, but women have done this before. I'll cope.'

'You don't want me to stay?' He would if she needed him. Practically.

'You've filled my freezer. You've chopped my wood. Why else would I need?'

There was no answer.

'You're leaving now?'

'I… Yes.'

'You want me to kiss you goodbye?' Her words sounded angry and he didn't blame her.

'I can do without it.'

'I'm sure you can. Thank you for the wood and for the food. And for my baby. Goodbye, Ben.'

He couldn't bear it. He crossed to the bed, stooped and kissed her.

Her arms didn't come out from the covers. She simply let herself be kissed.

'I'll be in touch,' he said helplessly.

'Lovely.' She didn't sound like it was lovely. It was the most perfunctory 'lovely' he'd ever heard.

'I'll transfer funds…'

'Thank you.'

'Take care of yourself.'

'And you.'

There was nothing else to say. There was nothing else to do. He turned and walked out the door.

She lay and stared at the door for a very long time. She'd sent him away.

If she'd clung…

If she'd clung he would have picked her up and carried her back to Manhattan and installed her in his sterile apartment.

'At least I'd see him.' She was very close to tears.

'You'd break your heart. You know it. Sit and write, he says, but how can I write fantasy when my hero's real and wants… I don't know what he wants. All I know is what he doesn't want.'

She let herself sob, just the once. If she granted herself more than once she'd be a mess for her entire pregnancy.

Speaking of pregnancy, oh, she felt sick.

'At least it gives you something to think about rather than Ben,' she told herself, but it was small comfort.

'This is going to be a great pregnancy,' she told herself. 'Come on, woman, pull yourself together. It's only two hours until you need to be at work.'

How many minutes thinking of Ben?

How many trips to the bathroom?

'It's hormones,' she said, clutching her stomach. 'I'll get over this.'

'Morning sickness or Ben?' She was talking out loud, a two-sided conversation. Heinz was at the foot of her bed, looking worried.

'Don't you look worried,' Mary told him. 'I'm worried enough for both of us.'

Why? She had herself under control—sort of.

Yeah, she was fine—except her stomach was heaving and the man she loved with all her heart was heading to the other side of the world.

CHAPTER THIRTEEN

HE DROVE TO AUCKLAND. He found a hotel, made a few international calls, did some desultory paperwork—and tried not to think about Mary.

Finally he met Jake. Hell, it was good to see him, but even though the warmth was there, he was instantly aware of tension. There'd been things unsaid since the cyclone, and they were still unsaid.

Maybe they'd been unsaid all their lives.

'Hey, Jake.' A man hug.

'Hey, yourself.'

They headed for a bar Jake knew, drank beer and pretended things were normal. But small talk could only take them so far.

After the cyclone there'd been the relief at seeing each other alive, but their mother's suicide now stood stark and dreadful between them.

But, then, maybe it had always stood between them, Ben thought. Maybe it had always stood between him and the world.

But now Jake knew the facts of his mother's death. Admitting it to Jake meant admitting its reality. Maybe Jake wasn't the only one who'd retreated to make-believe.

'I gather you're not just here to see me,' Jake said, as the small talk died.

'That's why I'm in Auckland.'

'That's not what I meant. Why come to New Zealand?'

'I brought Mary home.'

'Mary?'

'The girl who saved my life. She came to New York but was

ill so I brought her home.' There was a lot more he could say about that, there was a lot more he should say—*Jake was going to be an uncle?*—but right now he wasn't going further. He didn't know where to start.

But Jake knew him well. He was watching his face and Ben knew he guessed a little of what he wasn't saying. That something was wrong. That Mary wasn't just...the girl who'd saved his life.

'So now you're heading back?' His brother seemed almost wary.

'Yes. Tomorrow.'

'How ill is she?'

'She's okay now. Sort of.'

'And you're not getting involved any further?'

'I brought her home. In the company jet.'

Jake snorted. 'That's involvement.'

'Cut it with being snide, Jake.'

'I'm not snide,' Jake said, and suddenly he wasn't. 'I'm worried.'

'She'll be fine.'

'I'm worried about you.'

'Why on earth?' His twin's words brought him up with a jolt. Since when had Jake ever worried about him? It was *he* who did the worrying. It was Jake who got into trouble and it was Ben who picked up the pieces.

'I've met a woman, too, Ben,' Jake said, almost gently. 'Same as you, it's the woman who plucked me out of the sea. Only unlike you, I'm in it up to my neck. But...it's not going so well right now.'

Of course. He might have known. This was all about Jake. Of course it was.

He looked across at his brother's worried, open face, once more bearing tales of woe to his big brother, and something snapped. Here we go again, making him responsible...

'You don't need to tell me. Of course it's not going well. But there's no need to talk about it—I'll be reading about it in the glossies soon enough.' He sighed, raked his hair, feeling infinitely weary. Jake, alias Peter Pan, eternally young, good-looking, eternally flying from one disaster to another.

He'd had enough. He didn't have room for more emotion.

Jake was looking taken aback. Fine by him. It was time to tell it like it was.

'Maybe it's time you grew up, Jake,' he snapped. 'Marriages and happy endings belong in one of your movies. They're not the real world. Not for us, that's for sure. You've already tried and failed. You play-acted the perfect husband last time. Wasn't that enough?'

Jake was staring at him, dumbfounded. 'You think I was acting?'

But he wasn't shutting up now. He couldn't. 'You've acted all your life—just like our mother. You don't know what's real and not.'

'I wasn't acting the first time round,' Jake threw back. 'Believe it or not, I thought it was real. But now…I'm sure not acting this time. Ellie's different. She's one in a million. This is a million miles from one failed marriage.'

Enough. He'd had it, up to his neck. He was on his feet, his anger surging. 'Then you're even more of a fool than I thought. One in a million—just like the last one. And the next one and the one after that?'

'Will you cut it out?' Jake was also on his feet. The bar was empty save for a lone barman polishing glasses at the other end of the room. He was staring at them, making a tentative move toward them. Pre-empting trouble.

If they'd been ten years old, Ben would have been punched by now. Maybe he still would be. But as he watched, he saw his brother visibly force himself to relax. Jake waved to the barman, a gesture of reassurance, and when he spoke again his anger seemed to have faded. 'Ellie is different, Ben,' he said at last. He hesitated, as if searching for words, and what he finally said was confusing. 'And we're not…we're not our parents.'

What the…? 'What's that supposed to mean?'

'Just that.' Jake sounded as if he was figuring it out as he went, but increasingly he was sounding sure. 'We're our own people. You finally let it out, didn't you? In the life raft, when you said I wouldn't know reality if it bit me. That I was just like Mom. You told me she'd killed herself and you think I'm on the same path. Heading for self-destruction because I can't pick what's real or deal with it.'

'I don't—'

'Yeah, you do. It's gutted me, knowing now that Mom's death was suicide, but it's gutted me even more that you've kept it to yourself all these years. You've been protecting me, but you didn't have to. You've been protecting yourself and that's worse.'

'This isn't making sense.'

'Maybe it's not,' Jake growled. 'But this girl you brought all the way back to New Zealand. Mary. She went all the way to the States to see you?'

'So...what?' He couldn't explain. He couldn't tell Jake she was pregnant. One day soon he'd have to, but not now. It'd escalate this into the stratosphere.

'I'm not even beginning to guess what that was about,' Jake continued. 'But I don't have to guess because it doesn't make any difference. No matter who she is, no matter what she's done, no matter what she means to you, you'll never open yourself up. Because if you do then you open yourself up to that whole mess that was our mom. Our family. And Mom killed herself. Finally I'm seeing why you're so damned afraid.'

'I'm not afraid.' He was having trouble getting his head around this. Jake sounded sure of himself. He sounded almost... sorry for him?

'If you're not afraid of relationships, then why assume that whatever I have going on with Ellie will inevitably be another disaster for the glossies to gloat over?' Jake demanded.

There was a long silence. Jake turned away and stared out into the darkening night, and when he turned back to Ben his voice had changed again. 'Well, maybe it is a disaster,' he muttered, 'but at least I'm involved. I know I'm capable of loving. I'm not running away, like you.'

'Oh, for…' What was his brother on about? He'd never talked like this before. 'I'm not running away from anything.'

'It looks that way to me,' Jake said flatly. 'You run, you hide. Just like you've been hiding from me all these years by not telling me the truth. Shall we go there now, Ben? Talk about it properly? Or do you want to run away from that, too?'

How had this happened? He'd come to talk to his twin. His younger brother. What was Jake offering to talk about? A grief from twenty years ago? Any minute now he'd stick a counselling hat on.

In his dreams. 'I need to go.'

'Of course you do,' Jake said, almost sadly. 'People talk of emotions, you run. You've spent our lives accusing me of being like Mom every time I showed emotion. Play-acting. Yeah, okay, maybe some of it was, but not all of it. I'm trying to figure it out at last. Maybe the real is worth fighting for. The real is even worth hurting for.'

'Yeah, well, good luck with that. What did you say—that things aren't going well between you and this new woman? Amazing. I stand amazed.'

'Get out of here before I slug you,' Jake snapped, and as if on cue Ben's phone rang.

They both ignored it but it broke the tension. No one was going to get slugged.

No one was going to get counselled.

'Maybe you should get that,' Jake said at last. 'Maybe it's Mary.' Maybe it was. He checked.

'It's work.'

'There you go, then. I don't know why you're not taking it. Work's always been your place to hide, hasn't it, big brother? Why should anything I say make it any different?'

Which explained why he was back in his hotel room, staring at the ceiling at midnight.

There was a cold, hard knot in his gut that didn't let him sleep.

He could have flown out tonight. The plane was at his disposal. Work was waiting.

The conversation with Jake was reverberating in his head.

Mary was four hours' drive away. If he got on that plane…

'It'll make no difference if you go tonight or tomorrow,' he told himself. Work was waiting, piling up. He should go tonight.

He'd be walking away from Jake and his accusations.

He'd be walking away from Mary.

Mary.

She was in his head, brave, funny, alone.

She wasn't alone. She'd told him that. She had her community.

And a family who hated her.

Maybe he could head up to see her father tomorrow. Tell him what he thought of a dad who turned his back on his daughter.

Wasn't that what he was doing—turning his back on his child?

Mary's child?

'You've made the offer…'

Yeah, but it was an empty offer. He knew it. He thought of what Mary had here, Heinz, her nursing, her roller derby, her neighbours. She was coping with hate from her family but she was looking to the future. Her child could have… community.

That was what he didn't get. He'd never needed it.

Even in the army, Jake had embraced the life, enjoyed the communal living, found himself good mates who were still there for him.

He himself had been chosen for missions that had meant working alone. That was what he was best at. He depended on himself. Anyone else depending on him made him feel heavy. Some time, inevitably, he'd let them down.

As he'd let his mother down.

As he'd let Mary down.

He hadn't let her down, he told himself savagely. He'd done what he could for her. He'd always be there in the background.

Why couldn't he get her out of his head?

Jake's words kept replaying. He tried to stop them every way he knew how, but they were burned into his brain, on permanent rewind.

'No matter who she is, no matter what she's done, no matter what she means to you, you'll never open yourself up. Because if you do then you open yourself up to that whole mess that was our mom. Our family. And Mom killed herself. Finally I'm seeing why you're so damned afraid.'

Was he afraid?

'I asked her to marry me.'

'And that was opening myself up?' He was talking out loud. He had the penthouse suite in the best hotel in town. It echoed. There was no one to listen.

That was the way he liked it—wasn't it?

The night was doing his head in. His phone was sending a pale green light from its recharge station. He kept thinking of how Mary had been last night, wan and sick. He could just phone and check…

And do what? Say sorry you're morning sick or night sick or whatever they call it. Say call Kath if you get any worse. Say take care of yourself.

Take care of yourself… What hollow words were they?

'Maybe the real is worth fighting for. The real is even worth hurting for.'

Since when had Jake become a shrink? Hell, if he walked in Jake's footsteps he'd lurch from one emotional mess to another. He needed to get back to the States, immerse himself in his business world, forget this mess.

Was Mary…this mess?

Where was sleep when you needed it? Why had he scheduled the plane for ten the next morning? He needed to be on the plane now, heading back to his life.

His life without emotion. His life without mess.

His life without Mary.

He gave up on sleep, flicked open his laptop and started work. The figures danced before his eyes. If he made any decisions now he risked disaster.

Why could he not stop thinking about Mary?

It'd be different when he got home, he told himself. Life would get back to normal. He could forget Jake's extraordinary outburst. He'd done everything he could for Mary. She'd rejected most of what he'd offered but that was her call.

Her life was no longer his business.

Except she was carrying his child.

Except she was ill.

Except she might need...

Dammit, he was going nuts.

If he got up now he could drive there and back by the time he'd scheduled the plane to leave. He didn't even need to wake her. He could just check...and say goodbye...

He tossed back the bedclothes—and the phone rang.

Did death feel like this?

'Bring it on,' she muttered. Anything would feel better than what was happening to her body. Anything, anything, anything.

'I've called the ambulance.' Kath was there, looking frightened. She'd popped over just before dark, dying to talk about Ben, but she'd found Mary in a mess. Morning sickness had turned into afternoon sickness and afternoon sickness had turned into real trouble. Mary couldn't talk about Ben. She couldn't even think about him. All she wanted to do was die.

But an ambulance? For morning sickness?

'I'll be all right,' she managed, but they were a pretty thready four words.

'You'll be all right in hospital,' Kath said grimly. 'I'm thinking you haven't kept fluids down for twenty-four hours. Is there anyone you want told?'

But Mary couldn't answer. She was in extremis again.

She wanted to die.

* * *

Mary's phone. Mary? At two in the morning?

'Mary!' He almost barked her name, but the voice that came back wasn't Mary's.

'Ben? Ben Logan?'

'Yeah.'

'I've got the right Ben Logan? I'm guessing here. It only says Ben on the phone.'

'Yeah, it's Ben Logan.' He was almost shouting. Why was someone ringing on Mary's phone?

'It's Kath from next door.'

'Kath.' His heart hit his boots. 'The roller derby. The fall. She shouldn't have played.' There was a sick emptiness in the pit of his stomach. 'Has she lost the baby?'

And then came a worse thought, a thought that sucked the bottom from his world. Haemorrhage. Death. The words intertwined with such savagery that his breathing seemed to stop. 'Is she okay?' he managed, and he could hardly get his voice to work.

'She's not okay,' Kath said brusquely. 'But it's nothing to do with roller derby. The doctor's saying she has something called hyperemesis gravidarum. That's a fancy way of saying really bad morning sickness. Apparently she started being sick last night and she can't stop. She's had twenty-four hours' throwing up and she's got nothing left.

'I came by last night to see how she was doing without you and ended up calling the ambulance. She's in hospital now. I tried ringing her dad but her stepmum told me where to get off. I'm sorry but I work milking cows. I need to be at work in four hours. She's by herself. Not that she cares, she's too sick, but I thought someone ought to know.'

He sank on the bed as if dragged there by gravity. He felt sick himself.

She's by herself...

'How...how sick?'

'They've got a drip up but she's still vomiting. Sorry, Ben, that's all I know. Where are you?'

'In Auckland.'

'Is there anyone else I can call for her? I can't think of anyone.'

Of course she couldn't. There was no one.

'No,' he said in a voice that didn't seem to belong to him. 'I'll come.'

You couldn't hire a chopper at two in the morning, not unless you called out the army, and even Logan's influence didn't stretch that far.

He drove. He may have broken the speed limit. Luckily the roads were quiet. The big car ate up the miles while Ben silently went mad.

Mary was in hospital, ill. Mary was ill because she was carrying his baby.

Mary had…what had Kath called it? Hyperemesis gravidarum. He needed to look it up on the internet but he didn't have time.

Hell, why wouldn't the car go faster? It nearly killed him to slow through the towns. Only the thought of spending the night in jail with the car confiscated stopped him hitting racing-car speeds.

Mary.

Mary, Mary, Mary.

She could lose the baby. He'd accept that. He was making bargains, and the baby was his biggest offering.

'I don't mind,' he said out loud. 'As long as Mary lives.'

But he did mind about the baby.

His child. When had it become real?

Just now. The moment he'd heard Kath's voice. The moment he'd thought she'd lost it.

'Yeah, but I'm not giving my Mary up for you,' he told his unborn child, and he wasn't making sense, even to him. But he added a rider and knew it was true. 'I want you both.'

The road seemed endless.

He should have called Jake. Jake would have come with him. This sort of life-and-death situation, this race through the night, would appeal to his twin.

But it wasn't that. It wasn't Jake's energy he wanted now. He just wanted...someone.

He needed Jake.

He needed Mary.

And right there, right then, things cleared. It was like a fog was lifting.

He got it.

The offer he'd made Mary had been crazy. Nothing. It had been a dumb way to closet her neatly into the life that was already his. No wonder she'd refused, because he'd offered nothing.

He hadn't realised then what he was realising now. How much he wanted Mary. How much he needed Mary.

And if he wanted Mary he was going to have to offer a lot more than he had.

What had Jake said? *'I'm capable of loving.'*

'I am, too,' he told the night. 'Please, just give me a chance to show it.'

It was six in the morning when he finally reached Taikohe's community hospital. The nurse in charge took him into Mary's room but told him—sternly—not to disturb her.

'She's been retching for more than twenty-four hours. We've only just got her body to relax. I don't care who you are but if you even think of nudging her awake I'll send you into the middle of next week.'

Mary might not have family here, he thought as he followed the nurse, but she was right, she did have community. Kath had sounded frightened on her behalf. This nurse, who must know Mary personally, sounded fierce.

And then he was ushered into Mary's room and everything else was forgotten.

There was a low-voltage nightlight under the bed, casting a bluish tinge across the room so medical staff could see at a glance what was happening. It made the room seem weird, dark and yet not dark, surreal.

It made the figure in the bed seem...not alive.

He crossed to the bed in three strides, and then just...stood.

She was huddled under the bedclothes, tiny, insignificant, almost as if she was disappearing. Her skin looked almost translucent. That was the light, he told himself fiercely. She was...

'She's okay,' the nurse whispered beside her. 'This light makes everyone look like corpses. It scares the daylights out of our juniors when they first do their rounds. Not that Mary looks exactly pink and healthy but she'll be okay. Now we've stopped her being sick.'

He wanted to touch her. He wanted to feel her warmth.

Smash 'em Mary...what a joke. There was no strength in her. There were tubes attached to her arm, monitors, equipment he didn't know.

He wanted to gather her into his arms and take her home.

Home... Where was home?

Right here, he thought savagely. Home is where the heart is. Home was Mary.

'You want to stay?' the nurse asked, and he nodded. Where did she think he was going?

Nowhere forever, he thought. This was where he belonged.

Where was self-containment now? Jake would mock.

Let Jake mock. He drew up a chair and sat down. Let the whole world mock. Let his dumb armour fall away.

This was his woman, ill with his child.

This was where he belonged.

CHAPTER FOURTEEN

MARY WOKE TO SUNBEAMS, warmth—and someone holding her hand.

For a moment she didn't open her eyes. Why should she? The sun was warm on her face, she was cocooned in comfort—and the appalling sickness had receded.

Right now she felt...okay.

Right now someone was holding her hand.

'Hey,' a voice said gently. 'Hey, Mary, Smash 'em Mary, Mary my love. Could you possibly wake up? I hate to disturb you but apparently we have a date with an ultrasound in fifteen minutes.'

Ben was here.

She was dreaming.

She was so warm. If she opened her eyes the sickness could wash back. If she opened her eyes Ben would disappear into the dream this surely was.

'Mary,' he said again, and his voice was so warm, so tender, and the pressure on her hand was so gently insistent, that she had no choice.

She opened her eyes, and Ben was sitting by her bed, smiling down at her. He was smiling but his eyes were full of worry.

He needed a shave, she thought inconsequentially. He looked...haggard.

And then there was another thought, overriding even the amazement of Ben's presence. An appalling thought.

'My baby?'

Memory was flooding back. By the time she'd reached hospital she'd been in extremis. The retching hadn't abated. Her whole body had seemed to be rejecting her pregnancy.

Why had she stopped being ill?

'Is there something wrong?' she whispered, even though Ben was here. His presence was the most miraculous thing in the world and he was smiling at her and holding her but still… It nearly killed her to say it. 'Have I lost my baby?'

But… '*Our* baby seems to be doing fine,' Ben told her, smiling in such a way it made her heart seem to turn over. 'Except he's making his mother ill. The doctor says this doesn't mean a risk to the pregnancy. On the contrary, this illness means you're producing so many hormones that it's probably ultrasafe. There's nothing to worry about, Mary. Our baby's fine.'

There was a lot to think about in that statement. She was too tired to think much but there was enough to make her sink back onto her pillows and relax a little.

Her baby was safe, but it was *our baby*…

Ben was here.

'You…you're here. Why?'

'You scared the daylights out of Kath,' Ben told her. 'She told me she thought you were dying.'

Good old Kath. She remembered the fear on her neighbour's face last night and understood. 'Maybe I thought I was dying,' she admitted.

Why wasn't she ill now? She was scared to move in case it came back.

She wanted to close her eyes again but Ben was here and she didn't want to chance it.

'Dr Bolton says you were dangerously dehydrated,' Ben said. He sounded matter-of-fact but she knew this man well, and she could hear the tremor behind the words that said there was no matter-of-factness about this. 'Apparently there's a tipping point when you're ill. You get to the stage you're so dehydrated your body is ill because of it and the whole thing compounds into a vicious cycle. You went past that.'

'Yay for me.'

'I should have been here.'

'You're going back to the States.'

'Maybe we need to talk about that,' he said grimly. 'But meanwhile you have IV fluids topping you up and some ultrastrong antinauseant the doctor said he could give you, as long as I understood it's expensive. I've never been more glad I have money.'

She thought about that—and liked it. 'Me, too,' she conceded. 'You think you could put your fancy drug on the child-support expense list?'

'We need to talk about that, too,' he said. 'Mary, I drove for four hours through last night, thinking you might be dying.'

'That's bad,' she whispered. She couldn't get her head around why he was here. All she knew was that he was still holding her hand. He was right beside her, holding her, and he wasn't letting go.

'Mary, I don't intend walking out again,' he said. 'Not ever. Not if you'll have me.'

Whoa… These monitors should be bringing medical staff running with their crash carts, she decided. She was sure her heart had stopped, right there. She was struggling to breathe. She was struggling to take anything in.

If you'll have me…

'W-why?' It was a dumb question but it had to be asked. She felt out of time, out of body. This was happening to someone else, not Mary Hammond. Someone else was lying in a hospital bed, watching the man she loved with all her heart…

'Because I love you with all my heart.' His words were such an echo of what she was thinking that her dream seemed to intensify. The feeling that this wonder couldn't be real. But the pressure on her hand was real. The smile behind Ben's eyes was real.

And the look of fear that still lingered on his face was more real than she ever wanted to see again.

'I'm fine.' She put her hand up and touched his face. 'Ben, I'm okay. You don't have to do this.'

'Fall in love with you?' He shook his head and the fear faded a little. 'How can I not? I think I fell in love with you two months ago, right about the time you dragged me up a cliff in a storm. But it's taken me this long to acknowledge it.'

'So...' She was having trouble getting her voice to work, but she was really trying. Of all things, this was worth the most effort. 'So why acknowledge it now?'

'Lots of reasons. Because it took the thought that I might lose you to make me see. Because Jake called me a coward. Because you called me on being a twin, wearing this tattoo and yet not knowing what it meant. Because you've shown me what community means and how important it is.

'I've finally figured that community's great, I'll buy it, but family's more. I don't think Jake and I ever had a family. The way we were raised, with charades and bullying, we never knew what it was, but suddenly I'm seeing it and I want it. I want it with you, Mary. If you'll have me.'

There was something wrong with her eyes. Drat, they seemed to be watering all over the place. It must be the drips or the drugs or something because she never cried.

She'd never cried until she'd met Ben. Now tears were slipping down her cheeks unchecked and there wasn't a thing she could do about it.

'I can't...I can't live in that mausoleum of an apartment with a nanny between us.' She had to say it. She had to get it out there, even if it almost killed her to say it.

'I'm not asking you to. Mary, it took me four hours to drive down here. In four hours I've reorganised our lives.'

'Wow.' She was still so weak she could hardly take this in but she was trying. Oh, how she was trying.

'Mary, we can't talk about this now,' he said. 'You should be asleep. The doctors are wanting to do an ultrasound, though, just to make sure there's nothing wrong with our baby. Can you do that?'

'As long as I don't have to stand up.' Shock and weakness

were leaving her more than wobbly. If a faint breeze wafted through the window right now she might fly away.

'There's just one thing…'

'Mmm…?' He was still holding her hand. He was smiling at her as if she was the most precious thing in the world. The most precious woman… If this was a dream, she never wanted to wake up, she decided. She was staying in this place forever.

'I need to know…whether you can love me back.' And the fear was back in his voice. 'I know you said you loved me. I need to know…did you mean it? Because if you do, and if I love you, then the way I see it, everything else will follow. It's a huge step for both of us but, combined, our courage can face anything. You and me, Heinz and our baby, the four of us, forever. Do you love me, Mary?'

And there was only one thing a girl could say to that. This was important enough to wake up for. This might, just might, mean the dream could stay with her forever.

She put a hand up and traced the strong contours of his face. She touched his lips and it was as if she'd kissed him.

She loved this man with all her heart, and it was time to tell him.

'I do,' she said, and then she was being kissed and she couldn't speak for quite a while, not until the orderlies came to wheel her away for an ultrasound, not until the world broke in, not until dreams turned to reality. 'I do.'

He sat with her as the radiologist smeared gel over her tummy— a tummy that showed just the slightest suggestion of swelling.

For some reason his heart was in his mouth. When Mary had told him he was to be a father his first reaction had been of dismay. And fear. He wasn't meant to be a father. Ben Logan didn't do family.

Now Ben Logan was sitting by the woman he loved more than life itself—how did that feeling just keep growing stronger?—and he was praying their baby was safe.

He shouldn't have left her. For her to get so dangerously dehydrated this early in pregnancy… If her baby had died…

If his baby had died…

Their baby. His hold on her hand tightened. The radiologist noticed the grip and smiled.

'Scary, huh? You're about to meet your baby for the first time. I'll take photos—you can start boring the world from now on with pictures of your child.'

He thought, suddenly, of his parents. Two people totally caught up in their worlds. The thought of his parents ever showing friends pictures of their children was unimaginable.

They were selfish and self-contained. They'd done their best to destroy their children's childhood.

His mother's suicide had ended his childhood forever.

This baby would have a happy childhood, he vowed, and he'd be a proud dad. He would keep photographs in his wallet.

If things were okay…

'Here we go.' The radiologist was passing her wand back and forth over Mary's slippery belly and fuzzy images were appearing on the screen. A bean-shaped image. An image with tiny buds, hands and feet?

A face…definite symmetry. The beginning of features…

He was going blind staring at the fuzzy image. Mary's fingers were digging into his and her eyes were locked to the screen as well.

'Heartbeat's great,' the radiologist said, but her voice was strange.

Ben's gaze flew to hers. He was good at picking up nuances. There was something…

Back to the image… Her wand was moving back and forward. The image was shifting.

The baby had changed position?

Or not.

The image moved out. The bean-shaped image turned into… two beans.

Two heartbeats. Four tiny buds of arms. Four tiny legs.

Two heads, two hearts, two bodies.

Twins!

'Two,' Mary breathed, and it was half a sob. 'Are we...? Is that...?'

'Definitely twins.' The radiologist was smiling, the tension gone. 'Two lovely healthy babies with two healthy normal heartbeats. No wonder you've been so sick. Multiple pregnancies can be the pits for morning sickness. Is there a history of twins in your family?'

'No,' Mary said.

'Yes,' Ben said, overriding her. 'There's a very strong history of twins in our family.'

Our family.

Twins.

Mary.

If he got any more proud he might burst.

He had done some amazing things in his lifetime. He'd taken extraordinary risks. He'd had a fraught childhood full of stupidity. He'd fought in Afghanistan. He'd controlled the Logan financial empire with an iron fist and he'd made it grow exponentially since his father's death.

But he'd never been more proud of anything than he was right now, holding Mary's hand, looking at the images of his babies on the screen before him.

'Can we get two pictures?' he asked, and if his voice sounded choked he didn't care. 'One of each baby? I want one in each side of my wallet.'

One in each side of his heart, with Mary in the middle.

'You don't mind?' Mary said, but she was smiling and smiling.

'Mind? Why should I mind? We're having two babies. We need to get married right away,' he told her. 'Damn, I should have brought diamonds. How long before she's well enough to shop for diamonds?' he demanded of the radiologist, and she was smiling almost as much as he was.

'Now you're being treated things will be better,' she told Mary. 'And right now is peak for illness. By sixteen weeks the nausea should fade.'

'And looking like an elephant will set in,' Mary retorted, but her smile didn't fade.

'There is that,' the radiologist agreed. 'But if I were you I wouldn't let a bump, no matter how big, get in the way of a man buying you diamonds. That's just unasked-for advice from your elder, dear, so you can take it or leave it.'

'I think I'll take it,' Mary said, and suddenly Ben was gathering her into his arms, gel or not, wand or not, radiologist or not. 'I think I'll take it, if you don't mind. I don't seem to have a choice.'

Hideaway Island. A perfect Sunday afternoon.

They were sitting in front of their cave, looking out over the storm-ravaged island to the turquoise bay beyond.

'I'll buy it,' Ben said, and Mary blinked.

'Pardon?' It had been two weeks since the ultrasound. Ben had stayed on, working from Mary's tiny cottage, sitting on the back porch late at night, with Heinz at his feet, controlling the Logan empire online.

He'd have to return. They both knew it but neither of them talked of it. This had been time out for both of them, time for Mary to recover, time for Ben to take stock of his future, time for them to fall more deeply in love.

Mary had cut back on work but she still worked. Ben still worked online, but at night they lay in each other's arms and the world disappeared.

It couldn't disappear forever. This morning Ben had suggested they hire a boat and come out to the island, and she knew he wanted to talk. About the future.

About his sterile apartment with the nanny in between?

'I need to go back to Manhattan,' he said now, and her heart sank. Here it came…

'But I want to buy Hideaway first. If Barbara and Henry will agree.'

'I think they might,' she said cautiously. 'But…there's lots of upkeep. Are you thinking of visiting it, what, for a couple of weeks a year?'

'That depends on you,' he said, and her heart missed another beat.

'Ben...'

'Mary, listen.' He turned and took her hands in his. The sun was warm on their faces. Heinz was down on the beach, chasing gulls, turning crazy circles on the sand, as happy as a dog could possibly be. 'I've been thinking.'

'Dangerous,' she murmured, and he grinned.

'I know. It's scaring me, too. But I have a corporation to run and I can't ignore it.'

'I wouldn't want you to.' But was that the truth? Yes, she conceded. Ben was who he was. She wouldn't want to change a single part of him.

'The way I figure it, you have a community here but you don't have family,' he told her. 'In New York, I don't have either, but I do have my job. So I started thinking...could we build a community in New York? If we had family...we'd have everything.'

'A nanny's not a community, Ben,' she said bleakly, but it had to be said.

'Forget the nanny,' he told her. 'Dumb idea. There's two of us. If we can't cope with two of them, we're not the powerhouses I know we both are.'

'I'm not exactly feeling like a powerhouse,' she admitted, and he grinned.'

'Okay, nanny if necessary, just for when we need her. But you...you love your nursing?'

'I... Yes.'

'And your writing?'

'It's fun.' She didn't need the fantasy any more, she conceded, but she still loved it.

'And your roller derby?'

'It's awesome.'

'All those things are in Manhattan,' he said. 'We can find them. In fact, I already have.' He hauled a sheaf of paper from his jacket pocket and handed it over. 'The Manhattan Manglers practise four blocks from my…from our apartment and they're always open to new members. They seem to be mostly composed of young mums so team members come and go at need. You could, too.'

'Ben—'

'And district nursing,' he told her. 'There's such a need. New Zealand qualifications are recognised worldwide. You can do as much or little as you want. Manhattan will love you.'

'Ben—'

'And writing,' he said, trying to get it all out before she could object. 'I could take the kids out at weekends, giving you breaks while we bond. You could write all you want. And we can fix our apartment to turn it into a family home, or sell it and buy another if you want. And Heinz is okay to come—I've checked.

'And if we buy Hideaway we could come here for three months a year, maybe even more. I can work online. I can set things up so I train a decent second in command. I'll learn to delegate. I'll do whatever it takes, my love, for us to be a family.'

'You'd really want that?' she said wonderingly, and he tugged her close and kissed her, and then held her for a very long time.

'I want you more than anything I've ever wanted in my life,' he told her. 'I want my family. My last family was a disaster. I don't know if I can resurrect anything of my relationship with Jake—I surely hope so but for now it can't matter. All I know is that the woman I love with all my heart is in my arms. Mary, will you be my family? Will you be my community, my life, my heart? Mary, will you marry me and live happily with me for ever after, for as long as we both shall live?'

And what was a girl to say to that?

There was only one thing she could say.

'Yes,' she said, lovingly and firmly. Her answer rang out over the island where she'd rescued this man and he'd rescued her right back. 'Yes, my love, I will.'

* * * * *